THE SINGING STONES

Jeffrey Peter Clarke

THE SINGING STONES

FICTION4ALL

ISBN: 978 1 78695 292 9

Fiction4All
www.fiction4all.com

This Edition
Published 2020

Chapter 1

The valley lay nestled within a high land, rising to meet a sky of soulless embrace. A place laid wide to the elements where here and there, through a sparse blanket of greenery, earth bared her rocky bones. Amidst a domain of wind-scoured hills hidden ravines gave forth crystal waters from nameless regions, bubbling chill life until the hills reclaimed them once more in dark descent. Unfathomed, blank-eyed tarns rippled beneath blue skies and rolling clouds. Sometimes the mists gathered in secret council. Often the rains closed as curtains across an unseen stage. But on this day the world breathed raw and clear. Seen from above, sunlight bathed swarming metal ants, for the land was bisected, cleaved by a hairline ribbon of humanity, a main highway where busy people roared along in their wheeled cohorts with miles to dismiss, schedules to meet or hopes to fulfil.

***

Only a minute had passed since their vehicle left the busy main road and the world around was changing. They passed after further minutes along a deserted country lane that narrowed, imposed upon by overgrowing hedges, its once unsullied asphalt scarred by numerous potholes and pierced through here and there by the green claws of nature. Further on they reached a teetering wooden gatepost from which, its metal head bowed, hung a flaking green post box. Here they turned onto a dirt track, once, long ago, considerably wider but edged now by part tumbled rocky embankments. Their vehicle swayed and crunched wet grit on the deeply descending track. The man sitting next to the driver, clutching his briefcase, was inwardly apprehensive. Outwardly he was, when required, and would have to be on this looming occasion, the official. Always when required he was the official.

'There used to be a pub not two miles from 'ere,' said the driver. 'Maybe you'll remember it - the Coach an' 'Orses. Used to drink there with my mates in days past. Aye, nice old place it were, too - log fire an' all that, as well as good local ale. It's gone now, though. Aye, no more than a fond memory. These days there's nowt for six or seven miles, maybe more.'

'I wouldn't remember any Coach and Horses,' responded the official. 'I'm fairly new to these parts although it must be getting on for two years since I moved north.'

'It feels t'me even more like the back of beyond than last time we were 'ere,' said the driver. 'These people you're tryin' to sort out, I mean, they can't 'ave much of a life 'round 'ere can they – don't you think?'

'I don't suppose they can,' agreed the official, over the rise and fall of the engine, 'at least not the way most people look at things. We've discussed their situation at some length back at the office; we've tried to figure out how best we can help them. I've often been asked why they're so reluctant to move. And as you say, it can't be much of a life other than what most of us would regard as constant drudgery. Take away that old generator of theirs and

6

I reckon they'd be back in the Middle Ages. The council's offered them a fair choice of accommodation at reasonable rent, all with proper services - you know, central heating, modern kitchen, telephone, fitted carpets. You'd think at their age they'd welcome a chance to get away from good old-fashioned hardship and enjoy a taste of modern comfort. There are people who don't make any sense to most of us and never will. Oh well, I suppose it wouldn't do for us all to be the same – or so others tell me.'

'Well y'know what they also say,' the driver grinned as they descended the track, 'there's no accounting for folk is there – no, none at all.'

'You're right,' breathed the official, 'all too often there isn't and it doesn't make my job any easier.'

Where the ground levelled out they slowed and the driver, revving hard, shifted gear yet again to guide the vehicle through the churning black pools of a broad, rubble-strewn clearing. To their right appeared another wider but much overgrown track. The driver gestured to it, saying, 'Meant to ask last time I brought you up 'ere - where's that lead to? Can't be back onto the main road can it? It's goin' in't wrong direction.'

'Oh, that - yes, I recall it from our maps,' replied the official, 'it leads down and all the way around the back of the farm to the quarry entrance. I think this area must be where the workmen parked their cars.'

They left the clearing and continued, once more descending, along the rough track until the land again opened out. And now they had reached the valley, a sheltered area notably more fertile than the higher land through which they had passed.

'One thing I will say,' remarked his driver as the track began to curve around and the farmhouse with its huddle of outbuildings came into view yet further down on their right, 'it can be grand up in these 'ills on a warm summer day but very different in't winter if you've not experienced it. Looks very pretty 'round this part as well right now, but it must be 'ard life for anybody wantin' to 'ang on 'ere all year round if they didn't 'ave to. Why, as you say, when your lot are offerin' 'em the chance of a decent place in the village with shops close by.'

The engine revved once more. The vehicle rocked, creaked and lurched onward to trace a wide circle before coming to rest between the main house and a stone stable somewhat further away. Beyond, to the south, the land rose in natural limestone terraces before sweeping broadly down towards the curve of a distant reservoir.

'Quite so,' agreed the official once again as he raised a hand to prod at spectacles shaken down his nose by the motion of the vehicle. He gripped harder on the briefcase that contained the essence of his day-to-day working life, saying, 'Mind you, when I look at those outbuildings I think there must have been more than just the two of 'em living hereabouts in years past. A whole family, I'd say, or maybe they could have accommodated hired labour.'

Hugging a gentle grassy slope within the green valley, Lower Moss Farm and its several outbuildings grew from the land; limestone grey beneath shining roof slates. Amid the buildings a modest, sun-glinting lean-to greenhouse stood in contrast to muted stone. By one wall of the main house was parked a time-afflicted, drab olive four-by-four. On this occasion the driver saw fit to inquire, 'Which of 'em drives that old banger I wonder. Doesn't look roadworthy to me.'

'I really can't say,' replied the official, 'but I think it's probably him. They must use it to get their provisions. I can't imagine it ever goes far in that condition and I'd be surprised if the thing is even licensed let alone insured. That's none of my business I'm happy to say but I imagine it'll be left there to rot eventually with the rest of the place – if they take my advice and leave, that is.'

A short way to the north of this outwardly placid enclave spread a substantial grove of ash trees. No great distance beyond the trees the land arose steeply toward the bleaker Pennine hills, rearing as monstrous waves, stilled as they began to heave and pile upward in mid-rush to engulf all before them. Between the farm buildings and the trees lay a level, netted-off field where a stream-fed pond rippled and geese pecked busily about in the grass. Somewhat outside this area and higher up on rising ground, a small number of sheep stood in scattered indifference. Out of sight beyond the track and the farm, beyond the field to the north-west, lay the disused quarry that defined the boundary of a world the official was now intruding upon. The official had noted the quarry on council maps and although he had no interest in seeing it, its existence had been, in earlier days, of considerable importance.

'And you've still no idea why they phoned and asked you to come over 'ere again?' queried the driver.

'No, I have no idea whatsoever. I thought the last time would be it. If they don't see reason soon, they'll be left to get on with their lives as best they can. Trouble is, and you can bet whatever you like on it; if anything untoward happened to these people, accident or illness, we, the council that is, would be blamed for not doing enough to help. Yes, it'd be splashed all over the local papers.'

'Serves 'em right I say,' grinned the driver, 'but from what you told me of your last visit, it doesn't sound as though you'll see 'em out of there any time soon.'

'Possibly not,' sighed the official, reaching for the door handle in readiness to step out, 'but I doubt the powers that be will wish to waste any more time and effort here.'

The official was at once aware of a cool wind for it buffeted the car and hissed about the passenger door as he opened it. He stepped outside, buttoned up his jacket, reached inside the vehicle for his briefcase and paused for some moments after the engine died to stare with misgiving at the farmhouse. Through his mind coursed details of those previous attempts to have them understand what they had no desire to understand while the woman's gaze returned to occupy his thoughts. His last visit had been over a month before. Since then there had been another letter from the council delivered to their ancient roadside letterbox; an official letter in one of those regulation brown envelopes most people cared not to see. The letter had never been answered. People had no business in ignoring official letters. Perhaps it still resided damp and unopened within that rusted metal husk at the gatepost. But it was that last visit the official had most cause to remember. He recalled the drizzle and the chilling wind on his face. Chilling even in those later weeks of summer when elsewhere the fields were still green, the trees and hedgerows brimming life, the days still warm and mellow. It had been a final attempt to instil sense, official sense, into people who had precious little sympathy for the world of officialdom and its underlings. He had thought about it often since and now recalled tales of how, in the process of drowning, a whole lifetime might pass before a person's eyes.

***

'I don't like having to intrude upon you, Mrs Baxendale, but we are concerned that -.'

'Don't like!' she exclaimed. The ornately iron grated fire at the far end of the main room spluttered and spat as if in sympathy with her words as glowing logs settled. Mrs Baxendale fixed a harsh, pale blue gaze upon him, her eyes alarmingly magnified behind thick, circular lenses. 'Don't like!' she repeated. 'Well, just tell us – what 'ave *you* not got to like about it? It's not your ruddy 'ome they're tryin' to force you out of! 'Appen you wouldn't stand there lookin' so damned smug if it were!'

11

Tightly curled grey hair, a long floral cotton dress with wide collar and green cotton pinafore gave her the appearance of one yet to emerge from the realms of a bygone age; an age, perhaps, of post-war austerity. Her attire matched to staged perfection her husband's homely, comfortable armchair image. Mr Baxendale was a moderately flabby man whose once rugged frame appeared resigned now to the unpitying assault of time. His hair, thinning, smooth and grey, emphasised a round face of high complexion upon which glinted rimless spectacles. Stretching over a faded blue-striped shirt, well-tensioned braces supported baggy, brown corduroy trousers of some antiquity, the waistband gathered about a paunch nurtured over long years by a liking for warm ale.

Though of lesser height and of slighter build than her husband, in neither demeanour nor in speech did Mrs Baxendale make any concession to frailty. Her features might have been sculpted by the wind and rain; those same elemental forces that had shaped the Pennine hills that surrounded them. 'Granite with an abraded porcelain finish,' was how the official had once described her features and those same words passed again through his mind. More so even than those of her husband, her hands were hardened and callused by toil, her mouth set firm and determined. At all times did the woman appear determined, her unblinking gaze set as a mask of stern defiance. Mrs Baxendale stood a little forward of her husband. He had so far remained silent, drawing occasionally on the well-chewed stem of a rosewood pipe and dispensing acrid smoke that the official feared would persist to taint his clothes for days afterwards. Having so bluntly delivered her message, Mrs Baxendale, stepped abruptly back to stand at her husband's side and there waited in tense and challenging stance.

'Please,' the official insisted after this charged interlude, 'I'm not being smug about anything and we are certainly not and I repeat, *not* intending to force you out of your home. But I must try to have you understand the situation as a part of my job with the council. Mrs Baxendale, Mr Baxendale, I ask you again, with all due respect, to consider their proposition. With the quarry closed, the private road giving access to the track that leads to your property can no longer be maintained, not least because those few other farms in the area once contributing to it have also gone – unless, of course, you were able to support the entire maintenance cost yourselves, which I doubt you'd be in any position to do. This means vehicle access to your property will become more difficult than it already is and that is bound to affect any deliveries you may require. How this will also affect postal services I have no idea at all but there will be no services provided by the council. And as you're not online, as you don't have computer facilities, you'll still need to collect your pensions from the post office or bank and because of closures the nearest branch is several miles from here. Furthermore, most of this area is to be off limit to the general public because the quarry, so I'm assured, will become increasingly dangerous. Mrs Baxendale, Mr Baxendale, the assistance and accommodation on offer are most reasonable.

Please consider what I have said; I'm sure nobody wants to see you suffering hardship so I would rather you -.'

'Them int' council would rather we just walk out of 'ere,' cut in her husband, shaking his pipe stem at the official, who took a half step back to avoid flying droplets as Mr. Baxendale continued, 'Just give up our 'ome because some chinless little man int' town 'all puts his ruddy signature on a few bits of paper and says so!' The remark was followed by a wheezing intake of breath and a spate of sharp coughing before he jabbed the pipe stem angrily back into his mouth with a sharp click. Mrs Baxendale ignored the interruption, folded her arms defiantly and maintained an unblinking stare. Hers were hard eyes. Harder by far than her husband's. His eyes expressed no small measure of indignation but hers - hers were eyes that held a bitterness and resentment that went deeper than mere words could express. The official sensed an anger within her that might have welled from the unmeasured depths of a Pennine tarn.

'What do them in't town 'all know about folk like us - eh?' she demanded, 'What? Lower Moss Farm's *our* 'ome - *our* liveli'ood. This farm - aye, *this* farm and the land about it 'as been in my family for generations. That matters to us! Aye, we've worked 'ard all our lives as God above 'as witnessed and we've asked for nowt off nobody. No, we've asked for nowt! Never!'

'We've asked for nowt from nobody,' agreed her husband, adjusting the pipe between tobacco stained teeth with a repeated click, click, clicking the official found a source of considerable irritation.

'We owes you and them interferin' devils out there nothin'!' his wife continued. 'Tell 'im that sits on his damned be'ind all day and sends letters out *he* doesn't know what makin' a proper livin' is! Ask 'im why we're expected to move rather than 'ave them keep a bit of road in good order. If it were 'is 'ouse I'm sure it would be put to rights without a second thought.'

'Mrs Baxendale, Mr Baxendale,' breathed the official, striving hard to appear a model of self-control and conciliation despite inward feelings of a different nature, 'the council couldn't prevent them closing the quarry because it was owned by a private company, as you well know since it was originally your land they leased, nor can the council have any responsibility for maintenance of a privately owned road. All of this is determined by the economy of this area. I simply want to help you both to resolve a situation that we feel will become increasingly difficult and -.'

'Young man!' wheezed the husband, wagging his pipe stem yet closer the official's chest.

'Yes, Mr Baxendale,' sighed the official with his eye on the pipe.

'We understand the situation very well as far as you are concerned. We know the likes of you are just sent out to do the dirty work for them that doesn't dare show their faces - them that just sits shovellin' out letters to folk they 'ope they'll never 'ave to face in person. But 'appen me ant' wife ought to discuss things between ourselves a while.

Aye, sit thaself down while me and Elsie 'as a little chat int' kitchen. I'm sure you'll not mind waitin' five minutes or so as it must 'ave taken you a fair time to get all the way 'ere fromt' town 'all anyway.'

'No, please go ahead,' the official replied, wearily. 'I'll wait.'

He watched them walk around the solid old dining table and across the black-beamed room to the rear hallway and noted just beyond, before the door closed, a flight of stairs rising into shadowed obscurity.

'Dirty work?' he muttered. 'Face them in person? It's for their own damned sake I've been sent here – not for mine nor anyone else's.' The official regarded a rustic armchair positioned close to a shallow alcove built into the thickness of the wall between the main door and the window. He stepped over to the chair then, glancing at the door by which the two had just left, peered at the brown knitted cushion. There were vague stains but no crumbs and no hairs to be seen so, pulling the chair around and lowering himself carefully into its creaking frame, he sat close by the small, leaded window that was neatly framed by red and white gingham curtains. To the other side of the window stood a diminutive table on which rested an old black telephone with tarnished chromium dial. He imagined the telephone must no longer work as its owners had no listed number. He gazed across to high moorland and fading, treeless hills, some bearing the dark suture of part-tumbled dry-stone walls that retreated into the monochrome obscurity of a lowering mist. The weather even lower down in the valley could change quickly. Cold drizzle might sweep in from the surrounding hills and if the mist thickened the feeling of isolation would intensify. The vehicle in which he had arrived was visible from the widow and he could see the driver sitting inside browsing his newspaper. The driver would be waiting patiently. Perhaps in a while not so patiently. He listened intently but the voices in the kitchen were too low for him to make out what was being said.

There was within the room a pervading odour. Exuded by the very fabric of the house it was a hard to define odour of age, of old stone that somehow reminded him vaguely of a cathedral crypt. Under the low beams, opposite the window next to where he sat, stood an ancient, heavily carved sideboard, dark and solid. Upon it resided what in its day would have been referred to as a wireless set. In deep-lacquered wooden case with a curved top, intricately patterned front and Bakelite knobs, one of which was part broken away, it belonged to an age long departed and he wondered if it might be even older than the two for whom he now waited. He imagined hisses and whistles issuing from its dusty, valve-cluttered innards as its owners tuned in to hear in muffled voices, news of air raids over London followed by the measured gravity of one of Churchill's wartime speeches. He wondered if the radio would still pick up broadcasts. Did *they* refer to it as a radio? No it was definitely, it had to be, a *wireless*, and might now be a collectors' item even if it no longer worked. There was no television. This house could not possibly harbour a television. Its presence would surely be an affront, a blasphemy. Sharing pride of place next to the radio rested a large black and heavily embossed Bible with metal clasps and gilded page edges. He wondered which of these items they cherished most, the radio or the Bible. He decided it was probably the Bible.

Yes, apart from a parchment-shaded lamp that hung on twisted, brown flex from the centre of the ceiling, the old telephone and wireless set appeared to be their sole concession to the age of electricity. He could see no newspapers and no magazines; just a few cloth-bound books, possibly antique, slanted together on a sagging wooden shelf in an alcove to the left of the stone chimney breast. In the iron grate, the log fire hissed, flared and once more cracked. His gaze drifted up to the solid oak mantelpiece above the fire where a Victorian, ebony-cased clock ticked away patiently with spider hands quivering delicately over spider numerals. Perhaps the radio, the wireless, did work, or how would they know if the clock was showing the correct time? Perhaps it no longer mattered. He glanced at his watch and noted that the clock was some twelve minutes slow.

In the space to the right of the chimney rested a shotgun. Light gleamed upon cold iron barrels and the mellow polished timber of the stock. No doubt it had accounted for the fate of more than a few birds and rabbits in the fields and hills thereabouts. Looking up to the ceiling, he wondered what the two of them ever found to occupy their evenings in the gloom of those long and often harsh Pennine winters. 'Chatter to the sheep,' he heard himself mutter in an attempt to glean some humour from the situation. But this old house, the frowning moors and hills, seemed oblivious to witticisms. There were things here he did not and could never understand. Cosy the room might be but he found its oppressive out of time character quite alien. The stone walls, the old furniture; within them slept memories that might stir, might loom large in those isolated, confining hours of darkness.

At other times, when loosed of his official persona, the official had asked himself if these people were ever young. Had they, could they ever have experienced or enjoyed the wide-eyed novelties of scintillating youth? The question fascinated because even he, the official, had often laid aside his inhibitions amid the sunlit vistas of earlier years.

His gaze returned to where the black clock ticked away countless minutes. Interminable hours. Infinite days. What had it witnessed? What might it have to tell a world that no longer cared for the intricate, twitching microcosm that defined its mechanical innards? He thought uneasily that, if left alone here for long enough, he might fall asleep and awaken to find himself in another age. Then there was the disturbing sound he had noticed on an earlier visit – a mournful wailing carried on the wind like voices from the surrounding hills. He had never asked about the sound because he felt such curiosity might have compromised his image of detached officialdom.

Opening the briefcase he fingered through assorted papers, lifted out, regarded and replaced his mobile phone. That small item of day-to-day necessity, more so even than a television, might be a profanity in this house. He was fumbling in the briefcase for nothing more than reassurance. His official papers, his mobile phone - these things confirmed his place in a world that at present felt disconcertingly remote. His was a world of hierarchy, rules and regulations, a world of schedules, of meetings and digital communications, a world these people would doubtless find as incomprehensible as he found theirs. He abandoned his reflections, listened hard once again to their voices from within the kitchen, closed and lowered his briefcase to the floor. Their conversation, for the most part hushed and indistinct, was becoming now more audible.

Footsteps. The door creaked and Mr and Mrs Baxendale reappeared. Odd, he thought. It was as though he was encountering them for the first time. Perhaps it was because his mind had drifted, because he had allowed himself to become too relaxed. He now saw them as real people in need of understanding and help. This would not do. Any sympathies he might acquire ought to be, no had to be, set aside in the face of official procedure. He cleared his throat, arose from the chair and stooped to pick up his briefcase.

'Young man,' began Mr Baxendale in a low voice. The pipe had been placed aside. 'We'll not be talked into quittin' our 'ome by no one. No one -

whether you or them rudddy pen-pushers int' town 'all understands it or not.'

'If they wants to see us out,' put in his wife, 'they'll 'ave to break down't door and drag us through if that's what it comes to! We'll not give in to none of 'em, see!'

Another tense silence ensued. The official breathed in deeply. 'Mr Baxendale, Mrs Baxendale, I have to repeat yet again; no one is trying to see you out, as you put it. No, it's not like that at all and it *never* has been, but if that is the way you assess things then I'm afraid there's nothing more I can do to help. You understand, don't you, there will be no more offers of assistance from the council and that's really not what I wanted to tell you.'

'I don't give a bugger what you or any of 'em wants or doesn't want to tell us,' growled Mr Baxendale, 'and I don't see there's owt else to be said ont' matter.'

'Aye, we stay 'as we are,' affirmed his wife. She glanced at the main door, adding, 'So if you don't mind -.'

The official moved toward the door; a door of stout wooden planking that opened onto a small porch. There really was no more to be said as he laid his hand upon the heavy iron latch. From the corner of his eye he observed them standing together, their gaze fixed steadily on him. As he stepped out into the rain, there came from behind the voice of Mrs Baxendale. 'And close the door properly if you would!'

He glanced back into the house as he eased the door shut. It was her gaze he would remember. A gaze that might have turned him to stone.

***

On this his final, unscheduled visit the official regarded the briefcase in part as a talisman to reinforce his identity in the face of an anticipated hostile response. Above the valley, cotton-ball clouds drifted against a stark blue sky. 'At least it's not raining this time around,' he remarked.

'Best of luck!' came the driver's voice as his passenger moved away from the vehicle. On this occasion the sound of his slamming the door alerted the geese and from beyond the house arose a cacophony of cackling. He trod the grassy path toward Lower Moss farm noting that, on this occasion, there was no smoke visible from the squat stone chimney. The house appeared forlorn and had it not been for the riotous calling of the geese and a small number of sheep visible further out, an imaginary casual visitor might have thought the farm deserted. Behind him the engine revved as its driver continued around to complete the circle before switching off.

For a part of that short walk he was no longer the official. During those brief moments he was thinking, 'Do I want, do I need to waste any more time trying to help these damned people? They talk to me as if we were set upon persecuting them. And what's it all costing in time and trouble? Why don't they see sense, take the offer and get out for good? For Christ's sake do I need any more of this?'

He paused and looked about. He approached the house closer but could see no face at the window and no sign of the door opening. If anyone was at home they must surely have heard the vehicle and the geese. They must be aware of his presence. Once more the official, he stepped beneath the porch, raised his hand and was about to knock when he heard the latch click. The door swung inward and Mr Baxendale appeared with rosewood pipe planted firmly as before in his mouth. 'Well, well!' he exclaimed, raising his hand to swing out the pipe as if the visitor was unexpected, 'if it isn't the official gentleman from't town 'all. Do step inside, lad, won't you?'

With some relief the official noted in Mr. Baxendale's voice an absence of the hostility he had taken for granted would be in evidence. Stooping to enter, he found himself once more in that so familiar, so disturbingly cosy house, though his eyes took a few seconds to adjust to the low light filtering into the room. Mrs Baxendale emerged from the rear hallway to stand by her husband's side as before. Both were dressed exactly as he remembered them. In one hand she clutched the beige folder, containing details of the council's offer, left by the official on an earlier visit. The furniture and other items laid about the room, the feint odour of cooking, the yet stronger smell of pipe smoke as Mr Baxendale resumed puffing, the very essence of the place - it seemed as though only hours had passed, rather than days, since he had last stood there facing them. He summoned a half formal, half friendly, 'Good morning,' then decided he had no choice but to wait until one of them addressed him.

Behind them the fire gaped open and red, hungering for a few pieces of the chopped ash wood that lay neatly piled close by. Once fed, the fire would doubtless generate the copious smoke the official had noted was absent on his approach.

'Young man,' announced Mr Baxendale, detaching the pipe from his mouth with slow and studied deliberation. 'Elsie and I 'ave 'ad another look at the situation – aye, a thorough look, and we've made our final decision.'

The words, 'Thought they'd bloody well done that done that last time I was here,' passed through the official's mind.

'That is so,' agreed Mrs Baxendale with a deference for which the official was quite unprepared as she handed him the folder, 'Len and I 'ave decided to give up this 'ouse and farm as suggested but we'll not be needin' the council's 'elp.'

'Aye, we'll not be acceptin' the council's offer, kind as it were,' agreed Mr Baxendale. 'We'll be makin' all our own arrangements to move but first we'll dispose of our livestock - sheep, cows, 'ens an' all that. We've signed all them forms only where needed so you can 'ave a good look at 'em and take 'em back to the town 'all with you today.'

The official stared from one to the other, wondering if what he had just heard could be true and lowering his briefcase he affected a smile, accepted and opened the folder then as no more than a gesture he flicked quickly through the enclosed forms. He cleared his throat and announced, 'Er, yes, I'm sure everything will be in order – and, well, of course, the move will be left entirely to yourselves. But where d'you plan to relocate if you don't mind my asking?'

'For the time being,' replied Mr Baxendale, 'we'll take up residence at Elsie's sister's over in Yorkshire, she's plenty of room since 'er 'usband died and she'll be plenty glad of our company.'

'Look,' smiled the official, unable to remember if he'd had cause to smile before within those walls, 'let me say how pleased I am that you've made this decision. I am sure it will be for the best.'

'Well maybe - maybe not,' answered Mr Baxendale, pulling a worn leather tobacco pouch from his pocket. 'But at least it's settled and you people can get on with other business and forget all about us troublesome country folk.'

'When d'you anticipate your move will take place?' the official asked, though he cared not in the least.

'End of this month, lad, no later,' mumbled Mr Baxendale, gripping the pipe whilst stuffing loose tobacco into the bowl with studied care.

'Aye, end of the month,' agreed his wife.

'It'll be a sad day but there we are, that's 'ow things 'as to be. We'll take all our belongings - all that's worth owt anyway, and nature can take over t'rest.'

'Aye, a sad day,' concurred Mrs Baxendale as her husband seated the pipe to clicking comfort between his teeth and reached aside to the table for a box of matches, 'but we 'ave faith in the Lord and 'im above always looks after 'is own.'

'Aye, the Lord always looks after 'is own,' puffed Mr Baxendale with lighted match quivering above his pipe. The match expired, the pipe wagged but only a thin spiral of smoke ascended from it.

The official placed the folder into his briefcase and the pair stood watching as he moved to the door. He opened the door and turned for the last time to deliver his final words. 'Well goodbye and I do hope everything goes well for you both. And like I say, I'm sure you won't regret your decision.'

'I'm sure we'll regret nowt,' breathed Mrs Baxendale, her hand raised to push the door shut as their visitor crossed the threshold.

He might have expected to observe in those hard eyes a look of reconciliation but there was none. If that harsh voice and weathered stone face bore any expression at all it was one of tight-mouthed mockery. Behind her another match flared as Mr Baxendale strove to re-ignite the rosewood pipe after what was evidently his previous failed attempt. He was puffing harder, his teeth click-clicking on the stem as the door closed and the official, his attention firmly upon the waiting vehicle, stepped out of their lives forever. Behind him the latch also clicked - a note of finality.

'So you got away from 'em in one piece!' grinned the driver as the official adjusted himself in the seat. 'I take it they didn't 'ave the shotgun out.'

'No I'm pleased to say they didn't,' he answered, dropping the briefcase into the back of the car. 'And believe it or not after all the weeks of delay, they've actually decided to leave so that, as they say, is that, especially as they refuse all assistance from the council. I'll be glad to close the file I can tell you and I won't mind not having to face them again, particularly that woman. By god, she's a rum character!'

'Well there's a turn-up,' laughed the driver. 'So now we get ourselves back to civilisation and forget all about the place. And what about those cows I saw, the sheep and all them damned noisy geese - what'll 'appen there? Don't suppose they can take any of 'em onto a housin' estate.'

'I've no idea and nor do I care what will be done with anything,' came the reply. 'I imagine they'll have to sell the lot.'

As they jolted along to the ascending track the official glanced back at the receding farmhouse. It disappeared from view so he relaxed back into his seat and said, 'Don't ask me why but I get the impression there's more going on with those two than they'd want anyone to know about. The way she was looking at me you'd think they'd pulled a fast one. Still, they've made up their minds and that's all that matters. It's none of my business now - not any more it isn't.'

Chapter 2

He was a stranger in an unfamiliar town with time to spare after a morning of difficult negotiations with tiresome people in a soulless boardroom. Even the coffee machine had been out of order. Hesitating in the doorway to lower his briefcase and straighten his tie, he stepped into the busy main street, glanced at passing traffic, up at a leaden sky then down at his watch. 'Lunchtime and I'm free of the lot of 'em,' he breathed hesitating to look in both directions but for the moment uncertain over which way to go.

'Fancy a pint, old boy?' someone had asked him as he was about to leave the office. No, he had not fancied a pint. He had not fancied anything – at least not with any member of that particular crew, and being referred to as, "Old boy," when junior in years to some though not in status to any of them, he found mildly irritating. After his meetings with off-the-shelf people who ceased to exist after five-thirty, he was now to find himself adrift in a town where voices sounded different, where most of the street and place names meant nothing and where anonymous buses and Metrolink trams would be heading out with nameless people who, at the end of each working day, would disappear amidst uncharted grey seas of monotonous suburbs.

'Clucking old hens,' he muttered, glancing up at the window of the building he had just vacated. 'God, I could do with a drink.' He reached for his smart phone then changed his mind. It shouldn't be too difficult to locate a pub or wine bar so close to the city centre and at least the day was dry. The decision was made; he turned to the right, strolled along the road, glanced casually at shop window displays then paused at the first side street. Narrow side streets in city centres tended to harbour bars and restaurants and as this side street appeared promising enough he turned the corner to investigate. About halfway along he spotted the entrance to a wine bar called the Parakeet. On reaching this he stood to peer at its colourful avian device perched above the door then closer, briefly, at the lunchtime menu on display lower down. A glance through the window toward the bar opposite confirmed the place was busy but he expected it would be at that time of the day. 'Okay, looks good,' he breathed, pushing through the door.

He found himself confronted by a sea of busy chatter that all but overwhelmed a background of thumping music. He had progressed halfway to the bar when he glimpsed her from across the room. She was sitting at a small table in an alcove by the window with a cup of coffee poised in one hand. Odd, he thought, that he had not noticed her from outside when passing that same window only a minute before. The seat opposite to her was unoccupied. It was the briefest of glances but one that freeze-framed in his mind as he eased his way closer to the bar for she was young and strikingly attractive. There her image, persisting a while longer, might gradually have retreated from his thoughts, for that was what usually happened. It had been his intention, after a light lunch, to leave the wine bar with no particular aim in mind because his business affairs were on hold for the time being. Had he entered the wine bar a little later his day might have continued in the vague direction he expected as the seat opposite the girl would probably have been taken by someone else. He stood before the bar, located and perused in detail the lunchtime menu, placed his order, swiped his card and conducted only the briefest dialogue with the youth behind the counter who, obviously under considerable pressure, had too little time for casual discourse. The large glass of chardonnay was placed before him and the barman said, 'We'll bring your order over shortly, sir. D'you have a table number?'

He peered about the crowded room. 'Er, no I don't,' he replied. He could see no empty seat other than one by the main door where people would be pushing by so he had no wish to sit there. No other seat, that was, except for the one close to the window at the table where the girl sat. Thoughts tumbled through his mind. There were customers gathered about the bar, drinking, talking, laughing, some pushing closer and staring hard with hand part raised in an effort to attract the attention of the barman who presently awaited his decision. None of the people waiting there appeared a likely partner for her, although he might have found it difficult, had there been time, to explain why he had reached that conclusion. He turned to the impatiently waiting youth and pointed in the direction of the window. 'I'll make for the window seat over there,' he replied. It was that or remain standing amidst the crush of people close about the bar.

But as he weaved his way between the tables, glass in hand, doubts arose. Perhaps she was expecting someone - a boyfriend, a husband or maybe a business associate. His opinion inclined toward the last option because she wore a smart, midnight blue jacket and matching short skirt. That latter feature of her attire further sustained his attention as he approached the table.

He let his briefcase down to the floor, his hand alighted on the back of the empty chair but the girl appeared too preoccupied to notice his presence. On the table before her lay her cup, an opened magazine and next to it a plate containing a half-eaten sandwich. He leaned forward and cleared his throat. 'Sorry to bother you but, er, is this seat taken? It seems the only free one in the place.'

She looked up, her hazel eyes meeting his, her rose pink lips slightly parted. Honey blond hair spilled about her shoulders with a wisp brushing her cheek and, now close, he was aware of her exotic perfume. 'No - that's okay,' she replied, 'no one else is using it.' The hint of a smile touched her lips momentarily as she raised a hand to brush back the wisp of hair before turning aside to adjust the fawn raincoat she had draped over the back of her seat. She returned her attention to the magazine as he placed the glass on his intended half of the table, pushed the briefcase further into the alcove with his foot then sat down. He glanced at her and wondered if the seat had been empty because no one would think such an attractive young woman was likely to be in the wine bar on her own.

And though her eyes were fixed upon the magazine her curiosity was also taken by the arrival of the newcomer. She listened to the chair rattle and scrape, watched indirectly as the man positioned himself awkwardly in the restricted space between table and alcove wall. She noted his well-manicured hand as he steadied the glass of wine but she did not acknowledge his presence further. Her outwardly casual assessment had already confirmed him as an attractive male in his early to mid-thirties, his smart business suit quite possibly, no probably, that of a city professional. She was inwardly amused because she knew her presence must be dominating his thoughts while at the same time he would strive to appear indifferent. How could it be otherwise, unless -? She glanced at her watch, picked up the remains of her sandwich and wondered how long it would be before he summoned enough courage to initiate conversation. If it did not happen within the next few minutes she expected it would probably not happen at all.

He in turn felt he must avoid staring at her though beneath the jacket of her suit he had noted she wore a white, ruffle-fronted blouse over which hung, on a fine silver chain above her breasts, an engraved, oval silver locket of antique appearance. Her perfume further invaded his senses and spoke of exotic places. He drank a little wine, felt uncharacteristically nervous, wished he had a newspaper or magazine, anything upon which to concentrate his thoughts. The company papers in his briefcase did not appeal. There was the smart phone resting snugly in his jacket pocket. It was still switched on. From it he might conjure up something to occupy his attention. No, that would not do. He decided to fumble in his pocket and switch the phone off because there and then was not the time he wished to receive any calls. He found it irritating when people sat at the table stabbing at their little screens and chattering, and so he assumed others would find it equally so – and so might the girl sitting opposite.

He placed his glass aside and glanced at his watch to see it indicated a few minutes past one-o-clock. It might be a while before his modest lunch arrived; perhaps ten minutes, perhaps longer at this busy time of the day. He turned his mind with misgiving to the contentious meeting he had recently presided over, then dismissing this he looked through the window to see the sky had darkened and rain was beginning to fall. The flagstones of the narrow side road beyond were glistening wet and most of the passers-by had evidently done what he had not - set out equipped with an umbrella. That essential item was tucked safely away within the suitcase in his hotel room. Eyes still upon the scene beyond the window he sighed inwardly and the girl, seeming to sense it, glanced aside also to observe the grey street and overcast sky. She let down her still unfinished sandwich, closed her magazine and again peered outside.

The door of opportunity had opened slightly. But slightly was enough. 'Does it rain here as much as I hear people say?' he asked, determined not to let such a fleeting chance go by without at least a gesture.

The girl hesitated. Her inward amusement surfaced as a demure smile. The man opposite had made his move and would now be planning to build upon it. She looked at him and replied, 'I don't think so – no more than most places. I think it's the time of year.' Her voice was coolly musical.

'Do you, er, work here in Manchester?' he asked. He hoped the unaccustomed nervousness that beset him was not obvious to her.

'Work here?' she answered, sensing his unease. 'No, I'm visiting for a few days, that's all; just to see my parents.'

'Yes, me too,' he said, trying not to sound over enthusiastic now the ice was broken, or at least appearing to crack. 'Not to visit my parents I mean, but just for a few days. I thought you looked rather business-like and, er, I'm here on business myself as it happens.' She glanced once more through the window so he added, 'I've never been to the north of England before so - well, I don't actually know the city at all.'

'People usually refer to this as the Midlands,' commented the girl, coolly. At the same time she was able to fully assess his appearance: reasonably well-built and yes, good looking in a confident and refined sort of way with brown-eyes, short dark-hair, clean-shaven and smartly dressed in charcoal grey suit with plain blue tie.

'Oh, right, then the Midlands it is,' he smiled, 'but it feels fairly north to me because I'm based in the south; in London for my crimes.' His minor geographical oversight might have been a mountain but he had noted her modest suntan and so felt it appropriate to remark, 'You look as though you've been somewhere warmer and sunnier than Manchester. Have you just had your holiday?'

'No, I work abroad,' she replied, still intending to keep the conversation as superficial as possible as she finished the remains of her now tepid coffee.

'Work abroad - oh, do you.' his smile broadened. 'Whereabouts may I ask?'

'In the south of France: Languedoc, actually,' she replied, thinking now the wind of conversation was in his sails.

Further enthusiasm over the fact that she had responded to his question had indeed encouraged him greatly. The flicker of an eye had already confirmed that there was no ring on her finger so he concluded she was unmarried.

The girl had, of course, fully expected he would seek to develop their conversation further. But at that point their barely initiated dialogue was gate-crashed by the untimely arrival of his lunch.

'Would you mind taking these?' she asked the waiter as the fresh order was placed on the table.

The waiter clattered up her plate and unfinished sandwich, then her empty cup and the man now wondered if she was about to leave. But dialogue *had* been established and he had no intention of allowing it to lapse. 'And what d'you do in sunny Languedoc?' he went on, raising his glass to drink while having only a vague idea as to the whereabouts in France of Languedoc. 'D'you work for a holiday company? I get around Europe from time to time, mainly on business, but I've never been to your part of the world - well, Paris and Strasbourg a couple of times – I guess that must be the closest.'

She considered his question for a moment, gazing aside at the window as if to deny him any opportunity of insight into her thoughts. 'I'm personal assistant to the owner of a private organisation,' she answered at last, dabbing her lips with a serviette. 'It's a sort of health club. How about you - what kind of business are you in?'

'Oh, a very dodgy kind,' he replied, sensing in her manner a reluctance to offer more information about her own work as he added, 'at least that's what a lot of people seem to think. I'm involved in finance and investment - that sort of thing. I've been to a meeting at our branch office here to witness first-hand how they're coping with our affairs – or not coping very well at all right now.'

'Oh, I see,' was her only response as she continued to peer out into the street.

As he dealt with his own sandwich it occurred to him again that as she had finished her food and her coffee she would have no further reason to stay. She would get up and walk away and he did not want her to do that. If she was here like himself, on a visit, then quite possibly she also would be alone. He was anxious to finish his own food but felt that talking while eating would appear unseemly. He was anxious to clear the decks psychologically for verbal action and anxious to retain her attention. To persuade her to stay longer and continue in conversation was now his overriding priority.

'When's your return flight to France?' he asked. 'I take it you will be flying or – or will you go back by train?'

'The next flight to Montpellier is in three days. How long before you go back to London? That's where you said you we're from, isn't it?'

'That's it,' he smiled, pushing aside his plate of partly eaten sandwiches, 'the big smoke as they used to call it. D'you know London at all?'

'I've been there a few times - art galleries, museums, that kind of thing. I'm not really one for big cities.'

'No, they're not everyone's idea of fun,' he said, aware that he had not answered her question about the duration of his own stay in Manchester although he had planned on returning to London the following day. At that point he observed her reach down by the side of the chair to pick up her red shoulder bag and small blue umbrella. Placing these to one side of the table she appeared about get up and put on her coat. Too soon, all too soon, she was about to leave and he felt suddenly agitated.

'Er, look,' he said, raising a hand from the table, 'if you have a bit of time to spare will you join me for dinner this evening?' He surprised himself by the rash spontaneity of his own question and froze in anticipation of her response; a response that he at once concluded must result in the dismissal of his proposition and her inevitable retreat from the wine bar.

Her hand fell upon the shoulder bag, wide-eyed amusement lightened her face and he feared she was about to break into laughter. 'Dinner,' she began, 'god, I haven't the remotest idea who you are! You don't just sit down in front of someone you've never seen before and - and... or do you? Is that the way you operate?'

'Look,' he responded in the hope that his reddening face would not be as obvious in the subdued lighting of the wine bar as it undoubtedly would have been in daylight, 'I'm sorry if I sounded a bit out of place – no, look, entirely out of place.' He adjusted himself uneasily in the chair, attempted to relax then added, 'I didn't mean to appear pushy because I – I'm not trying to - but we're both visiting Manchester and, well, I'm at a bit of a loose end so I thought if you were as well, then - then maybe you wouldn't mind - perhaps.'

As his voice trailed off the girl looked at him with a perplexed smile. She regarded his ill-concealed unease with renewed amusement but it was oddly reassuring because it suggested he was more a spontaneous opportunist rather than one of the numerous calculating predators she had encountered too often in the past. Letting the shoulder bag rest on her knee for the moment, she asked, 'D'you make a habit of inviting complete strangers out to dinner when you're away from home? Is that your style? And d'you have a wife sitting at home in London wondering when she'll see you again?'

Mustering what he hoped was a reassuring air of laid-back humour, he answered, 'No, I really don't have anyone at all waiting in London and I don't make a habit of chatting up complete strangers. Tell you the truth on this occasion I just thought I'd -.' He shrugged then added, 'Sorry I really was out of order.'

'So there's no one waiting for you,' she said. 'Oh, well, I suppose that's something at least.'

He leaned back, awash with regret at his foolish proposal as she pushed away her chair. She was standing now and smoothing down her skirt as women often do when they are about to set off. Looking aside she lifted up, shook and pulled on her coat, picked up her bag, slipped the strap over her shoulder then collected up her umbrella. She was aware from the corner of her eye how he stared at her newly vacated chair, to the window then down at the table but his words paraded large in her head.

Never a man to contemplate defeat, never one to back down, he was now telling himself he should never have gone near the table but stayed at the bar to mind his own business. He hoped no one had overheard their conversation, that no one was aware of his failed attempt to gain her acquiescence. Failure he always considered a burden carried by other people. He turned again to the window where her vague reflection was evident and wondered if she might bother even to say goodbye before stepping away when the sound of her voice touched his ear. 'Where did you have in mind for dinner?'

'Sorry?' he responded, taken aback as if not fully comprehending her question.

'For dinner - where did you have in mind?'

Pushing back the chair, he arose to face her, his mouth widening to a boyish grin. 'Well, I er - I don't have the slightest idea but - but there must be dozens of good restaurants in a town this size.'

'Yes, I dare say there are,' she said, coolly, whilst eyeing his expression of revived optimism to her own inwardly broadening amusement.

'Then, em – okay, how about eight o'clock right outside here?' he said, gesturing with his hand to the window. 'I'll have a table booked somewhere decent nearby and organise a cab to get you straight home afterwards. Oh, and by the way, my name - it's Richard.'

She took the hand he offered and smiled with calculated reserve, 'Yes, that's a point isn't it - names. I'm Karen.'

'Well, Karen,' he began, 'thank you for – well, thank you. I do appreciate this and I'll certainly look forward to seeing you at eight.'

She smiled briefly then stepped away from their table. Richard watched her make her way across to the main door, her slim, alluring form his only object of interest in that crowded bar. He sat down, turning his attention once more to the window, expecting to see her pass by outside with her umbrella raised but much to his disappointment he soon realised she had not taken that direction along the street. Yet for a while longer he continued to watch with her image and her words dominating his thoughts. He turned away from the window, picked up his unfinished glass of wine, downed the contents, sighed aloud and smiled with self-congratulatory satisfaction.

***

Her eyes reflected the light of the candle nestled within a red crystal globe at the centre of their small table. His spirits were high and the world was a better place because she was sitting there with him.

Only a half hour earlier his mood had been very different. Then he had stood waiting in the street, as arranged, close to the wine bar where they had met. The night had been damp and cool though the rain had ceased earlier. The much-anticipated hour of eight o'clock had passed, though only by five minutes, but she had not appeared. He had begun to wonder if she would keep their rendezvous then he had stepped over to the wine bar thinking perhaps she had misunderstood him earlier and gone inside to wait. Yes, that would have made sense so he had glanced through the window to check the table where they had sat. The wine bar was not as crowded as before and the table in question had stood unoccupied. By ten past eight, he had all but convinced himself she would not keep her promise and that it had been a foolish mistake to expect her. The image of her smiling face, a burning beacon in his thoughts, now was dimming to an empty husk. Twice as the minutes passed, as he strolled up and down by the wine bar, he had considered walking away, walking on to tread the short distance to the main road where he would call a cab or maybe drift amidst head-bowed people and deserted shops before returning to a soulless hotel room. Twice he had changed his mind, one voice within telling him to be patient and wait a while longer, another deriding his own gullibility in expecting an attractive young woman to meet with an all but complete stranger at night in a darkened side street of an unfamiliar city. When eight-fifteen had passed

41

he turned for a third time, intending now to leave. Then footsteps. The hurried click-click-click of high heels on cold flagstones. Stepping out to the kerb, he had seen a figure approach from the direction of the main road. A figure barely illuminated by the streetlights, muted by the darkness but wearing a pale raincoat with a shoulder bag swinging at her side. His heart had quickened.

She had apologised for being late. She had caught a bus instead of a taxi and misjudged the time it would take to return to the wine bar. Richard had affected his broadest possible smile and assured her it didn't matter in the least because being late was a lady's prerogative. No, he had assured himself as they walked on, it didn't matter in the least.

'Well, Karen, what d'you think of the restaurant?' he asked now they sat facing one another. 'Does it meet with madam's approval?'

'I think it's a lovely restaurant,' she smiled, taking a sip of aperitif sherry, 'lovely and warm as well after being outside. I take it you haven't been here before, or have you – I mean when you've chatted up other women?'

'No this is absolutely the first time, and I did tell you the truth. And as I also said, this really is my first trip up to Manchester and I've had to rely on my smart phone at times to get around. I asked the receptionist at my hotel to recommend somewhere with good food and not too noisy. She told me she knew of a place near St. Ann's Square and this is it.'

Even as they had entered to walk down the winding stairs and into the small, discreetly lit warmth of the cellar restaurant with tables clustered beneath a vaulted ceiling, he had determined that Karen would be more than just a passing acquaintance. She would be more than just a casual encounter - job in France or no. He had determined it even before she slipped off her raincoat to reveal the black shoestring dress that fitted her alluringly curvaceous form like a glove.

Karen's trip to visit her parents had demanded nothing out of the ordinary as far as style was concerned so she had purchased the dress and the strappy high heels in one of the city's fashionable shops that afternoon and laid aside her two-piece suit. The dress was short but not too short. Karen wanted to enhance but not to advertise herself though she had given little thought as to how far the two concepts might overlap. Transitory encounter with this man or no, Karen, like most women of her age, wished to be admired. She felt confident about her new male acquaintance. Confident enough to take advantage of his company and determined to make the best of her stay in the city should their acquaintance continue.

Richard had noted her small earrings of spiralling silver and above her breasts there still hung the silver locket. If before he had considered her beautiful, he now regarded her as exquisitely so, and very desirable. The tribulations of that morning had vanished as chaff in the breeze and Richard now considered himself king of the evening.

Karen in turn appraised Richard's finely tailored suit and blue silk tie and concluded they did not originate from the rail of a high street chain store. If he was keen to impress her he had at least made a promising start.

'Now, what about you?' he continued. 'You mentioned your parents live outside the town; d'you often make it back over here to see them?'

'This is my first visit since I went to work abroad,' she answered, feeling at ease in the reassuringly cosy intimacy and cool, big moon over the city, jazz that she found so agreeable. 'I've been away from England since early last year.'

'And will you fly back there direct from Manchester?'

'No, I'll have to return to London by rail then it's another train to Gatwick airport.'

'It might take longer travelling back to Gatwick than it takes to fly out to the south of France – d'you think?'

'I never worked it out,' she replied, 'but I suppose there won't much difference if you take into account the time we all have to spend queuing to clear security.'

'I guess I'm fortunate, if you care to look at it that way,' he continued. 'Once I'm home I only have a twenty-odd minute overcrowded journey to the office by tube. I dare say you don't have any of that to contend with over there.'

'No, I don't,' she breathed, 'and I don't think I'd care to, either.'

Earlier that day in the wine bar he had asked her about her work and Karen expected sooner or later she might have to face more questions. At that moment the waitress loomed, seemingly from nowhere, to hover at their table and for a time they were occupied with the menu. On making her choice, Karen noted the prices and concluded Richard must benefit from a generous expense account.

'D'you have a liking for Champagne,' he asked.

'Of course I do,' she smiled, 'I work in that part of the world where they make it.'

While Richard was concluding their order, Karen thought briefly over her situation. The short time spent with her mother and father had been far from easy. Even in childhood she had never felt close to either of them, and her adolescent years had been spent mainly in the stultifying confines of a Catholic boarding school. In travelling up from London, she was doing little more than to fulfil a minimal duty, which in part was why she had accepted Richard's invitation. She too had been alone with little else in mind when he had appeared at her table in the wine bar. He had struck her as both confident and good-humoured in spite of his faltering efforts to proposition her earlier that day. It had amused her. She had wanted to laugh at the awkward expression on his face but there was no doubt she found him physically attractive. That he was an opportunist was obvious enough from the start though she suspected also that his disappointment would have been entirely genuine had she refused him. But then Karen understood the male of the species better than he could have imagined.

When the waitress had departed Karen said, 'You never told me earlier when you have to go back to London. I did ask you, didn't I?'

'Yes, I remember you did,' he replied. 'Well it's a bit open ended, actually. I'm due for a break so I hadn't really made my mind up and -.' He hesitated and placed both hands palm down upon the table. 'No, look, I shouldn't be telling you that because it's not altogether true. I was thinking I'd probably leave tomorrow but it's really up to me. I do have some time owing and it's quite flexible as I'm a senior partner in the company. I suppose you already have a return ticket - or do you?'

Karen sensed the stirring of another proposition as she peered at him over her raised wineglass. 'No, not exactly,' she replied, 'the next flight is in three days but I haven't actually booked anything. We're, em, yes - we're both telling fibs aren't we, Richard.'

'Guilty as accused,' he grinned, 'so now's a good time to stop. So tell me, when *are* you going back to France?'

'I will be returning, yes, but I haven't quite decided when and that really is the truth.' Her fingers touched the silver locket and remained there several seconds as she added, 'But I don't feel it matters an awful lot just now.' Karen realised her action had drawn his attention to the locket so she removed her hand aside. Richard possibly had guessed how important it was to her and was wondering if it contained a portrait of someone very close. His next remark confirmed that. 'I see, then you – you do have someone over there.'

'Yes, I suppose I -.' Karen hesitated then sighed. 'It isn't as cut and dried as that, Richard. Few things in life ever are, are they, but it is a part of the reason I flew back to England and why I didn't buy a return ticket. That's really all I have to say about it.'

An awkward silence was ended when a metallic rattling announced the arrival of a waiter who placed a condensation-beaded bucket supported by a chrome stand at the side of their table. From the bucket protruded a champagne bottle. A loud pop followed. Karen watched Richard raise a prohibiting hand above the newly opened bottle as he nodded his thanks to the waiter. Richard, it transpired, did not like anyone other than himself to pour wine at the table. 'So,' he resumed as the waiter stepped away, 'as well as seeing your parents you came back to get a few other bits and pieces, personal things, sorted out; is that what you're saying?'

'That's about it, I suppose - yes, to get myself sorted out if you want to put it that way. But I didn't join you for dinner to offload my problems, for what they're worth. What about you, Richard? You seem to be something of a free spirit. I take it you really aren't married, as you said earlier, or have you changed your mind?'

Richard lifted the moisture-hazed bottle from its bucket and filled their glasses until champagne foam oozed over the edges. Karen studied his face intently as he replied. 'No, what I told you was the honest truth; I'm not married. I confess I've been close to it a couple of times over the years but well, you know, things happen – or in my case didn't happen. I reckon the kind of life I lead probably has some bearing on it. It can be a bit hectic now and then, especially when I'm flying off at short notice to sort out problems with our branch offices, like this morning. It can be twenty-four hours a day when things get a bit pushy and I have to admit that wouldn't suit a lot of people. Ah well,' he added, holding out his glass to click against hers. 'Cheers - I dare say where you live there's plenty of decent champagne and good food on offer as well as plenty of time to enjoy it.'

'Cheers,' replied Karen, adding, 'Yes, Richard, as it happens there is good food and as I mentioned, lots of champagne.' Each savoured the wine then Karen said, 'Your terribly busy life didn't stop you finding time to chat me up though, did it?'

'No,' he smiled, 'I'm delighted to say it didn't. I haven't lost touch entirely with the real priorities in life. Well - not yet, anyway. And now we find ourselves here I'm truly glad you accepted. Yes, good wine, good food and the company of a beautiful lady are exactly what I needed.'

Karen returned his smile, saying, 'Hm, an interesting order of priorities, Richard. Still I'm glad I accepted. I am enjoying our evening and I needed this break as well.'

'Then we both did the right thing,' he responded. 'But tell me, will you be catching the train back to London soon? I take it you didn't plan to hang around in Manchester for much longer.'

'Oh, another day or so,' she answered. 'In fact, as we've decided to be honest, I'll tell you my little secret. I have a small, furnished flat at Notting Hill. I took it a few days ago on a monthly basis. I confirmed the agreement online less than a week before I left France. It isn't much, really – just part of a terraced house but plenty big enough for one person and it's close to the Central Line tube station. I didn't feel I could stay up here with my parents more than a couple of days – no, it isn't easy. Apart from that, I wanted to see a bit more of London.'

'Notting Hill,' he responded, 'my company has a suite at a hotel just along Bayswater Road for out of town visitors. Some of us make personal use of it on the odd occasion - when it isn't booked that is. One of the perks of the business, you know.'

'One of quite a few perks from the sound of things,' said Karen.

'All right, I suppose there are a few. Anyhow, when we're both back in London maybe we could meet up for dinner and I'll book us in for a West End show. Would you like that?'

Karen stared at Richard for some moments before answering. She was only just getting to know him and he was forging ahead at a rate she considered not altogether acceptable. 'We'll see,' she answered, quietly. Here was a man who was evidently used to getting his own way.

'I'm rattling off at a tangent, aren't I,' he grinned, 'but, hey, what about tomorrow? Do you have any -?'

'Richard,' she interrupted, 'I'm not sure we ought to let this -.'

'Karen, look, I – oh, Christ I'm sorry,' he responded, hands raised in a modest posture of surrender. 'I'm being too pushy again and it's quite out of order. It's not fair of me to expect you to go along with, whatever - with someone you only bumped into a few hours ago. Really, I -.'

'No, Richard, I understand. It's not entirely your fault. It's just that things aren't all that easy for me though I do appreciate this lovely evening, really I do.' She thought for some moments then added, 'But go on - what were you going to say about tomorrow?'

'No, I'll keep it for later,' he replied. 'You tell me about the part of France where you work. Tell me about the countryside, the people, the food and wine - anything you want; I'm all ears and I won't bore you with my business affairs.' He glanced aside, eased back in his chair then added, 'And talking about food, it looks like ours is about to touch down.'

***

It was close to eleven-thirty when they departed the plush comfort of the restaurant to face the chill air of a late-night street, now almost deserted. A muffled pounding of rock music seeped from the depths of a cellar bar on the opposite side of the street. Beneath a dark awning close to the restaurant they hesitated and there they kissed for the first time. Karen was willing enough, her hands resting lightly then tightening on his shoulders as his arms slipped about her slim waist inside the perfumed warmth of her raincoat.

'Look,' he said, feeling the sensual heat of her breath tingle his cheek but withholding the words of intimacy he wanted to utter but dared not. Nor did he wish to utter those words he did speak. 'I'd better organise a cab to get you home then I'll wander back to my hotel. I guess the walk will do me good.' He expected he would all too soon be alone with nothing other than memories.

'Richard,' she breathed, now regretting she was about to see him cast adrift, 'thank you for this evening. I've loved every minute, honestly - but I'll sort out my taxi. I can't let you pay for that as well.'

'That's not the point,' he responded, 'the evening's on me and by that I mean *all* of it. It's my way of saying a big thanks to you for agreeing to keep me company. You didn't have to say yes but it really has made my day.'

Another kiss and she asked, 'How far is it to your hotel?'

'Oh, maybe ten minutes, no more than that. I can organise a taxi for you there if you're happy to walk that far with me. It would make things easier since the cabbies are lined up nearby and there certainly don't seem to by any around here.'

'Yes, okay, I wouldn't mind a bit of a walk either.'

They started toward the main road then hesitated. As Karen turned to face him, Richard placed his hands on her cheeks to speak the words he had only minutes before suppressed. 'Karen, when we get back to the hotel - I mean will you -?'

For eternal seconds she gazed into his eyes. He feared she might now turn without another word and leave him standing there. He feared it until she answered his question in a whisper. 'I know what you mean, Richard. And, yes, I'll go back to the hotel with you. Yes, I'll go all the way.'

His heartbeat had quickened as he asked, 'What about your parents – won't they be concerned? It's quite late now.'

'I told them not to worry if I didn't make it back there tonight. They have my mobile phone number if they feel they need to contact me but I very much doubt they'll bother.'

Arm in arm they trod the darkened street to the main road and it no longer mattered that a light drizzle had resumed. For Karen it was a return to the summer evenings of warm breezes she had left behind in France. For Richard the sun had already risen and was shining brightly. Neither had spoken when they reached the bright lights and welcoming foyer of the hotel. As they walked to the lift the smartly uniformed girl behind the reception desk smiled at Richard. Karen wondered if this was simply a gesture of politeness, a corporate requirement or a knowing look to indicate she had observed him pass that way before with a previous casual conquest.

They entered his hotel room and Richard switched on the main light.

'Hmm, rather posh isn't it,' Karen remarked as her high heels plumbed the depths of a sumptuous muted green carpet. She peered around the interior of a suite obviously intended to satisfy the requirements of those willing and able to pay, and remarked, 'It's easily big enough for two. And you've had this all to yourself - or have you now?'

'I promise you I have and it's all arranged by our company secretary. I have to admit, though,' he confided, glancing about the ornately elaborate furnishings as he helped her off with her coat, 'neo-baroque, or whatever it is, isn't exactly my taste; I prefer art deco.'

'Well I'll put up with neo-baroque if there's nothing else around,' she said, slipping off her shoes. They kissed and Karen added, 'And I take it the bathroom mirror has a heavy gilded frame with vine leaves and cherubs because it's where I'm heading next if that's okay.'

'It's right over there,' he assured her with a gesture. 'And that part of the suite is definitely twenty-first century.'

Karen stepped into the bathroom. The lights burst on to reveal a warm world of mirrored, chrome-glinting, towel-draped luxury that boasted an extravaganza of toiletries and cosmetics in opulent array on glass shelves together with a display of colourful plants in floor-standing Chinese vases. She paused before the big, circular mirror, passed a hand over the sensor and on came the peripheral lamps. 'Wow,' she breathed, 'I'm a star.' She regarded her reflection, teased away hair from her cheek then looked aside to where cosy dressing gowns hung and the spacious shower area beckoned.

'I'll call for more champagne if you fancy!' came his voice from outside the bathroom.

Karen peered around the doorway. 'Richard, no! If you don't mind I'd rather not have any more to drink this late at night but I am going to try out this super shower if that's all right with you.'

'No problem, and I'm sure you'll find everything a girl could want in there.'

When some twenty minutes later she emerged from the bathroom in pink woollen bathrobe Richard, seated in an armchair and wearing just his shorts, looked up from his financial paper. 'Hey, Karen,' he declared, 'you're the birth of Venus.'

'Not the Botticelli version, I hope,' Karen responded, 'I dare say his Venus had a pretty face but she was a rather odd shape. I prefer a more conventional approach to the female figure, possibly Manet or Moreau. I completed an art course in my teens, you see.'

'Oh, cultured as well as beautiful,' he grinned, rising from the chair to cross the room where he slipped his arms about her waist and kissed her on the lips, adding, 'Well I don't know all that much about Manet and I never heard of Moreau but you're real enough and that's all that matters – and I reckon you'd put any of their efforts in the shade.'

Karen smiled but as she placed her hands on his chest the smile faded and her voice was grave, 'Tell me now, Richard, what d'you expect from me, apart from the obvious?'

'Karen, love,' he answered, slipping his hands from her shoulders then stepping back with a shrug, 'you say that as if I've set out deliberately to place you under some kind of obligation. I do hope that's not how it seems.' Her question had caught him off-guard. In his mind there had never been any doubt as to how their time together in his hotel room would progress.

'I *am* under some kind of obligation, Richard,' she replied, thrusting her hands into the pockets of her gown. 'I put myself under it quite willingly by returning here with you because I really enjoyed your company. What I'm asking is - is what d'you expect from me eventually – I mean after tonight?'

'Okay, for now your company and after that – well, I hoped we'd stick together for a while, one way or another. No, I mean for more than a while if that's at all possible; and I hope it will be.'

'But I'll probably be returning to France,' she said, 'and you will certainly be going back to London in a few days to carry on with your business.'

'Of course, and I'm being pushy again I know, but – but surely we can arrange something, though can't say what at this precise moment. It would be great if maybe – if maybe I could fly over to the sunny south of France and join you there for a while. You could show me around then later on you could come and stay with me in London. I'd be happy to arrange everything. The one thing I want to do is give you a fabulous time.'

'That's very sweet of you, Richard, but let's not plan too far ahead. You hardly know me so it may not be such a good idea.' The smile returned as she added, 'And have you seen the time?'

Richard eyed the bedside radio and said, 'Ah yes, I guess it's past our bedtime. Lights off now, d'you think?'

55

'Yes, Richard, lights off now,' she said, stepping to the bed where she placed her locket and chain on the bedside table before slipping off the bathrobe to reveal a beguiling nakedness. Mesmerised by the sight of her, Richard hesitated before switching off the lights.

In the intimate, sealed-bubble sanctuary of the hotel room their cries of ecstasy arose, spiralling to vanish amidst shadowed corners as each drank in full from the chalice of pleasures. Drank until it was emptied dry and set aside to make way for contented sleep.

***

Richard awoke to music spilling from the clock radio and there she was by his side, her eyes still closed, her lips slightly parted, her honey-blond hair delightfully cascaded about the pillow. Sufficient morning light filtered through the window blind to gently illuminate the room. The sound of early rush hour traffic rumbled subdued from beyond double-glazed windows and the clock radio glowed seven thirty-two. 'God, I'm glad it wasn't just a dream,' he muttered, pushing upright against his pillow to gaze down at her. Karen stirred and opened her eyes. She had awoken some minutes earlier and was fully aware of his presence.

'Would you care for a coffee?' he asked as she eased herself further up her pillow. 'I can call for breakfast as well if you'd like that. The food here is not at all bad.'

'Oh,' she smiled, 'I'm sure the food is perfectly wonderful if the rest of this hotel is anything to go by, but I was never one for breakfast in bed. I'd

56

rather shower and get dressed first if that's all right with you.'

'Fine by me,' he replied, slipping from the bed to part open the window blind. 'D'you want to go in there right now?'

'I really don't mind if you'd rather go before me,' she answered. 'I can hang on here and read the hotel magazine.'

'Or we can be good environmentalists,' he grinned. 'We can run the shower just once and do our bit to preserve the planet.'

'What! You mean you're not going to take a shower? Well I certainly am!'

'No, I mean we shower together – you know, to save water. It is a wet room, a luxury wet room at that, so there's plenty of space in there.'

She began to laugh. 'Richard, you are so funny!' He leaned over the bed to kiss her, and Karen said, 'All right then, I'll be a good environmentalist as well but I get to use the luxury hotel shower gel first – okay!'

***

A world away yet not so very far, a Pennine wind sighed. It sighed across hills that arose dark against lowering clouds. It sighed about fields and sheltered valleys. It sighed around the cold limestone walls of an old farmhouse that, should anyone care to make enquiries, was long abandoned. It sighed, too, above a deep, deserted quarry where, in shadowed depths, a terrible secret lay.

57

Chapter 3

The little corner café was pleasantly light, cheerful and replete with potted plants and coloured blooms.

'It's more like a greenhouse isn't it,' Karen remarked in a whisper when they had been presented at the table with their modest order of croissants and coffee.

'We could have taken breakfast in the hotel you know,' said Richard. 'They wouldn't have bothered in the least over my having company. I don't think anyone does nowadays.'

'Perhaps you know more about that than I do,' responded Karen. 'You say they wouldn't bother but I'm sure they'd have stared at us when we weren't looking and passed silly comments even if they are used to men like you bringing back their women friends at night. You know what some people are like. Anyway, at least in here no one will think it odd that I'm wearing a raincoat to cover this black evening dress.' Karen looked about, adding, 'Yes, I'm happier in here with the plants if you don't mind. They don't have opinions on anything – at least I hope not.'

'I don't mind at all,' he answered. 'And I wouldn't mind either if you and I visited a few other places while both here, I mean, 'ere oop north, as they say - if you can spare the time that is.'

'It's still the Midlands, Richard,' she corrected, peering at him over her coffee cup. Karen suspected Richard would be planning something further and he in turn knew she suspected it. He noted the faint glimmer of amusement in her eyes when he asked, 'Look, em – as neither of us has any definite plans how d'you fancy a day or two away somewhere different? We could just set off into the wild grey yonder. Maybe we could head over the hills towards Lincoln. I hear it's a great town to visit and I know for sure we don't have a branch office there to distract me. I checked the route and road travel time on my phone while you were getting ready and –.'

'Oh, did you now!' she interrupted. 'How very thoughtful.'

Richard stared down at the table, twitching his thumbs together and thinking, 'Christ, Richard, keep your mouth shut.' But after seconds of charged silence Karen said, 'Well, go on then.'

'Ah, right,' he said, feeling a surge of relief, 'it ought to be an easy journey over the Pennines but if it looks like it's getting too late we can stop off at some village or other where there's a small hotel or a pub. Shouldn't be too difficult finding accommodation this time of the year. What d'you say?'

Karen considered his proposal and mused, 'Hmm, we have been a busy boy haven't we.'

They had spent the night together and they had been intimate again in the confines of the wet room that morning. It was some time since she had enjoyed sex with a man as much as she had with Richard but though confident enough over his intentions Karen wondered how much further she should allow this brief though so far highly agreeable relationship to go. Then again, did it

59

matter? She had only one more thing to do before going back to London. No one would be waiting for her at the flat in Notting Hill but there were decisions beyond her return there to be considered. She remained silent for a while, gazing through the window, then said, 'I've not been to Lincoln since I was ten or so. It was a coach outing with my school and I do remember some of it - the cathedral, the castle, the city walls and all that. Yes, it's a lovely old town.'

'Does that mean you'll go along with my brilliant idea?' he asked.

'Let me think about it during the day and -.' She swirled the remaining coffee around in her cup then said, 'Oh, what the hell - yes, Richard, all right, let's do it.'

'Great! Then why don't we aim to be there early this evening. We could have dinner and stay overnight.'

'I can't make it today, Richard, no. I promised to take my parents out this evening. It's their wedding anniversary and I haven't bought them anything yet so I planned to do a bit of shopping this afternoon. Anyway, all my things are at their house; my clothes, make-up – everything I'd need.' She noted in his eyes the unspoken question before adding, 'but after today I'll be free - if you're still going to be around, that is, and as long as you let me chip in toward the cost. It isn't right for me to be relying on you all the time and I really mean that. I may not be a part of your business executive crowd but I'm not hard up either. I do hope you understand.'

'Well - sure, if you insist. Meanwhile, I'll get onto the office in London and let 'em know I'm staying up here a day or two longer than planned. I said I was due for a break, didn't I, so I'll get back to my hotel and have them organise a hire car. D'you want to meet me at the hotel for lunch around one?'

'I'd prefer it if we met for lunch again in the Parakeet,' she replied, 'since we both know exactly where it is.'

'In the wine bar it is then,' he agreed.

***

Richard switched off his phone. It was done. They had expressed little surprise when informed that he would not be returning directly to the London office and they had assured him there was no pressing need. Of Karen and their intended journey he had of course said nothing. The car would be delivered to his hotel by eleven o'clock the next morning, Wednesday. He had ordered a medium sized hatchback. Too extravagant a car, he suspected, was unlikely to impress her - perhaps just the opposite. Apart from what she had already told him, Karen did not appear to be short of money and whatever business she might be involved in abroad intrigued him greatly.

Having changed and intending soon to take his newspaper down into the hotel bar, Richard stood with comb poised before the bathroom mirror. 'We've made a good start there, matey,' he informed the image grinning back at him. 'Yep - she's one foxy lady and well worth the deficit we're going to make in the company expense account!'

He much regretted that Karen was unable join him that evening. It would instead be his financial newspaper for company and dinner for one.

***

Though in the company of her parents, Karen, too, was alone. Their reminiscences, their concerns, their opinions; none of them shared the paths she trod. Before the years she had spent at boarding school a rift had been growing between them. Now it was a void across which the wings of sympathy and understanding had not the stamina nor the desire to fly.

In the carvery of a traditional country pub, her crinkle-haired mother had questioned her about her plans for the following day in the same way earlier in the week she had questioned her about her occupation in France, openly but from different angles and with a none too subtle attempt to prise open the sealed vessel of Karen's personal affairs. Her conversationally detached father had refrained from prying and appeared interested in little else other than cricket - a sport that Karen, when her father began to voice his opinions over the current progress of the England team, would happily have relegated to the abyssal depths of the ocean. She thought it odd neither of them had questioned her about her evening away from the house or about the briefly alluded-to friend she was intending to visit the following day. Perhaps they realised that pursuing these subjects would achieve nothing.

***

She did not intend to be late a second time. It was nearing one o'clock when, attired in her blue two-piece suit and fawn raincoat with shoulder bag at her side, Karen entered the Parakeet wine bar clutching a holdall that contained everything she would need for the excursion with Richard and for her eventual return to London.

The wine bar was not quite as busy as it had been on the day she had first encountered Richard but the table by the window where they had sat on that occasion was occupied. Karen had expected to see him waiting by the bar but as he was not she peered about the room then concluded he was yet to arrive. A small table stood free beyond the end of the bar. It occupied a shaded corner but had a good view of the window and of the door letting onto the street beyond. She stepped across to place her holdall down by the table, slipped off and draped her coat over the back of the chair then made her way to the bar where she ordered a large glass of sauvignon blanc. She returned to her seat, expecting Richard would appear long before she had finished the wine. She waited, taking her wine slowly, determined to make eye contact with no one. The music was too loud - pounding rock music that Karen found increasingly irritating. She asked herself why – what was the point in it? She glanced at her watch. It was almost a quarter past one. She thought of the mobile phone in her shoulder bag but realised neither had given the other a contact number – no, they had not even exchanged their second names.

The bar had become busier, the chatter noisier with the entrance now obscured by customers, and still Richard had not appeared. Karen for a time had assured herself something must have happened to delay him. Richard had not struck her as the type who would pretend to make elaborate arrangements in order to deceive. But, how could she know after such a brief affair what kind of man he really was? She began to think that perhaps he'd had all he wanted out of her after what must have seemed an easy pick-up. Perhaps he was already on his way back to London - but then there was the expensive hotel suite. It made little sense. She was aware of two men at the bar looking across at her. Glancing at each other then back at her. One was grinning. Both were talking as if they wished not to be overheard but Karen imagined the gist of their conversation.

By one twenty-five with hands clasping the wineglass, her impatience had given way to annoyance. Then annoyance to anger. Anger with herself rather than with Richard. Sitting conspicuously alone with an almost empty glass and surrounded by groups of anonymous people in a bewildering sea of chatter, Karen made her decision: she would wait ten more minutes and no longer before getting up and leaving. She would return to her parents' house, book an on-line ticket and make the train journey to London next morning. There she would arrange her flight and spend two, maybe three more days at her flat before returning to France.

The two men at the bar were glancing at her again. Perhaps she would leave the wine bar sooner than intended and so she finished the remainder of her wine. Karen was about to rise from her chair when she glimpsed him hurrying by the window. Entering the bar, obviously out of breath, Richard pushed through the crowd while peering anxiously about. Failing at first to see her in the darkened corner he stood with a look of angered resignation clouding his features until she waved to attract his attention. He stepped across, rattled back the chair opposite her own and sat down heavily.

'Karen, love, I'm really, really sorry I kept you waiting like this but I legged it here quick as I could.'

'What happened?' she asked, realising something important must have intervened to delay him.

'We had another problem at the office – something I might have foreseen but unfortunately I didn't. There's still some damned stupid disagreement amongst senior members of the staff with one of them threatening to quit so I've been held up there trying to sort things out. I couldn't get away until now and – and we never swapped phone numbers did we, otherwise -.'

'That's okay, Richard, I assumed you'd make it here sooner or later.' Karen smiled, not wishing to have him suspect how close she had been to quitting the wine bar. The music and chatter seemed to recede as she asked, 'Have you sorted all their problems out now?'

He reached out to squeeze her hand. 'No - look, I'm afraid I haven't sorted them out and I have to get back for another meeting before two-thirty, and then I'll need to spend time talking to our people in London. That means I - that means we can't get away this afternoon. Karen, look, I'm really sorry for messing you about like this and it's certainly fouled things up for me.'

She forced another smile, saying, 'Oh well, I suppose these things happen,' and hoped her voice did not hint at the disappointment she felt as she added, 'The trip was a nice thought.'

'Karen, look, our trip doesn't have to be off. We can still go but it'll have to be later today than I wanted; much later, I'm afraid - if that's all right with you.'

'Oh, later - how much later?'

'I can't say right now, not exactly, but it may not be until after we close the office at five-thirty, and I do appreciate this time of the year the evenings are starting to close in. If I'd realised something like this was brewing up, I'd have arranged for us to get away earlier then we'd have been well clear of the damned lot. Mind you, I guess they'd still have been chasing me on my phone.' He gazed hard at her. 'I - I suppose I'll have to accept it if you change your mind but – well, the car is arranged as I said it would be.'

Karen thought for some moments as he waited for her response. 'No, Richard, I won't change my mind; that wouldn't be fair if it's not your fault. I suppose I could have lunch here, wander round the shops and spend the rest of the afternoon in the art gallery. My only problem is that.' Her gaze fell upon the holdall. 'I'll have to lug the holdall around with me.'

'Ah, don't worry about that,' he assured her with newly kindled enthusiasm, 'I'll take your bag back to the office; it'll be perfectly safe there. I'll bring it straight around to the hotel and meet you at six in the reception - how's that sound?'

'All right, you're on,' smiled Karen, extracting her collapsible umbrella from the holdall and wriggling it into her shoulder bag.

'We'll have a cup of coffee at the hotel bar,' he continued, grinning broadly, 'then we'll be off. Tell you what, though, they've had it if they want to get hold of me after today. I don't care if the damned office burns down. They won't have a clue where we are and my phone will stay switched off - I promise! And here's another promise,' he declared, getting up from the table then leaning to kiss her on the forehead, 'Tonight I intend to buy you champagne and the best dinner you've had since - well, since whenever!'

'You mean since last night,' she responded with a wide smile as he collected up the holdall. 'And I'm supposed to be on a diet.'

***

Richard arrived at ten minutes past six with the holdall to find Karen seated in the reception. She wore her blue business suit and the white ruffle blouse and there as before glinted her silver locket. On the chair beside her rested the fawn raincoat and red shoulder bag. Mid-September twilight descended earlier that day because rain was falling so they did not delay for coffee at the hotel. They drove from the hotel car park and nudged out to be swallowed by the morass of late rush-hour traffic. Through the hiss - click, hiss – click - hiss - click of the windscreen wipers, Karen watched the city-

67

centre lights drift hesitatingly by. They were carried along at sporadic pace through a canyon of offices and shops engulfed within a light-pulsing metal glacier where traffic lights, under the control of a malignant power, seemed forever to glare red.

'Did you straighten your work problems out in the end?' she asked as, with the engine sound rising and falling, they edged along.

'Straighten them out?' he replied, hesitating to glance at the small screen of the satnav as the bland female voice instructed him to turn right at the next junction. 'Yes, I reckon I did – or at least for the time being. Nobody wants to take responsibility for anything if they can offload it onto the likes of me. Coming here from our head office it's - well it's like being an emissary from some medieval pope. They want me to decide who's a heretic and who's a true believer. I won't go into boardroom, or should I say boring room details, but with a bit of initiative and a few cups of coffee they could have worked their way around the problems in less than half an hour. Instead, they foul up my – *our* entire day.'

'Most people prefer not to take responsibility, Richard - don't you think? You're from the head office, as you say. Perhaps that's why they look to you for advice.'

'Oh, I suppose you're right,' he breathed, edging the car around toward the next set of traffic lights, 'but I feel they could try a bit harder on occasion and forget their petty jealousies. Sometimes you have to sort yourself out, you have to see what's needed and just get on with it. If we all stood waiting for somebody else to help us over every hurdle we'd never start the race, let alone finish it. That's the way I look at it, anyway.'

'Not everyone can do that, can they,' she responded. 'You're self-confident – you're well set-up work-wise and financially secure so you can do more or less what you like. You're a high-flyer, Richard, like a lot of the people I've encountered during my time in France. God, the world some of them live in - even you might be surprised by it.' She now regretted having spoken those last few words. They were an unintended verbal bait and Richard would doubtless be tempted to find out more. 'There are other people - lots of other people,' she continued, 'who try hard and work hard but circumstances are against them. Some have strings of qualifications after their names but end up filling shelves in supermarkets or serving in bars like the Parakeet. Can you or anyone else say it's always their fault if there aren't any decent opportunities on offer to them?'

'There's usually something if you try,' he answered. 'There's often a way around things if you have the will power and maybe a bit of imagination. You did, didn't you; you got yourself a nice little number in the sun from what you've told me. That's because you made the effort and climbed out of a hole when most people would have stayed there complaining. A lot of 'em just sit there feeling sorry for themselves and do nothing. Now it's me should be sorry,' he added. 'I'm grousing because it's something that's taken up a good part of my day and landed us in this damned awful jam.'

Karen gazed through the rain at a kaleidoscopic river of traffic. Brake lights and flashing indicators, red, green and amber signals telling people to stop, go, stop, go, stop, go when for much of the time they could go hardly anywhere at all. Richard pulled the hand brake on and cursed quietly.

'I don't think what you said is altogether fair,' Karen remarked at last. 'From what you told me I suspect you fell on your feet. I'm not saying it isn't because you don't work hard or because you aren't clever - I'm not saying that at all. But you must have had your share of luck as well. As for me – well yes, I suppose I was fortunate in many ways. When I decided to take my chance and leave England I felt I had nothing to lose - no, nothing at all really. But anything might have happened - I might have ended up in - well, never mind.' Karen reflected upon her life in France but would say no more about it.

Richard turned to her saying, 'I guess I do sound a bit smug. Sorry, Karen, I don't mean to be. I know there's little confidence or security out there for a great many people. Maybe it's what helps to keep my side of things going – we take chances with other people's money and charge them for doing it whether they win or lose. But I still say you have to make the best of things, even so - like this damned traffic. Maybe there'll be something on the radio we can listen to. What sort of music d'you like?'

'Oh, I like classics, some jazz and a few other things but not that music, or whatever you want to call it, in the wine bar. How about you?'

'Sure - jazz, classics, that's okay by me.'

Richard stabbed at the radio screen. There were voices. He stabbed again. There was music and Karen said, 'That's fine if it's okay by you.'

'It's fine by me,' he smiled.

'Which way are we headed now?' she asked, glancing at the satnav but unable to make out meaningful detail.

'It looks like we follow signs for Stockport,' he answered, zooming out the touch screen map while they were again held up by the traffic lights, 'then we head roughly south-east over the Pennine routes. Maybe our little friend here will get us out of this sooner by taking us through the back roads. I have to tell you, though; we might be computer dependent for most things but I've less faith in modern technology than a lot of people. There's too much to go wrong. What I mean is, when it lets you down it can be a very big down.'

'We can't do without it nowadays, can we,' Karen mused. 'It rules so many people's lives.'

'Yes, so many people's lives,' he agreed, 'including mine. We'll need passwords and usernames to brush our teeth and put our shoes on before long.'

'Mm, well, if technology helps get us out of the city quicker I suppose we shouldn't complain. If it was daytime, I'd look forward to seeing a little of the scenery but as it's already starting to get dark I suppose that's out for today at least. How about you - do you mind driving at night?'

'No, I don't really mind as long as I can get a move-on,' he answered. 'Once we're out of this chaos the rest of the journey should be reasonably easy. Ah, I think we're starting to shift again. Who knows,' he quipped, 'we might be out of here this side of midnight then I can really put my foot down! I should tell you now, young lady,' he grinned, 'I'm still a boy racer at heart.' As they moved forward he glanced again at the small screen then aside at Karen. 'Technology or no, you can still help by keeping an eye on the road signs so I don't miss a sudden turning. My eyesight isn't all that good for longer distances - too much time spent in front of the screen staring at figures I guess.' In that sideways glance he had once more noted the locket. He concluded that, because she wore it at all times, it must mean a great deal more to her than mere adornment and yet again he wondered why.

In time, with music and light conversation to help alleviate the journey, they were clear of the city and heading out through an unappealing sprawl of twilight suburbs toward open countryside. Soon the world would be widening, soon the road would be ascending to higher lands. Karen relaxed, closed her eyes, listened to the music and thought over what had happened since that lunchtime when she had sat alone by the window in the Parakeet wine bar only to be approached by this now familiar stranger. For now, she was contented.

**

The city lay far behind and they had entered a more elemental, a starker reality. Rain, frantic myriad sparks of cold fire whirled from an infinity of darkness, pirouetted in the headlights, speared at the windscreen then darted away into hostile night.

'Remember what I asked you when we first met in the wine bar?' Richard asked after minutes of concentrated silence.

'Er, oh, you mean about the weather,' answered Karen, gulping back a yawn as she gazed through half-closed eyes. She had felt mesmerised by the hiss of wheels on the wet road and the rhythmic darting and whirring of the windscreen wipers. 'Yes, I do remember. You asked me if it rained all the time here, didn't you – or something like that.'

From the radio there were voices, though Karen had not been listening. Then more music and she found herself wide-awake once more.

'Yes, something like that,' he replied, peering hard into the night. 'But I think the question's been answered. I enjoy driving but I'm never too pleased when it turns out as bad as this.'

There had been few lights in front or behind for some time on that stretch of the road and yet fewer vehicles passing in the opposite direction. Now there were none.

'It doesn't seem as bad as it was earlier,' Karen remarked after more minutes had passed. 'Or am I imagining things?'

'No, it's definitely easing off as we get higher,' Richard answered. 'D'you want to check the weather forecast on your phone? I've not managed to hear any of it this last day or so and we've missed the news.'

'I can't get at my phone from here with my safety belt on,' she replied, glancing over her shoulder. 'My bag's out of reach on the back seat.'

But the rain had lessened now to a point where the wipers were intermittent.

'Never mind,' he said, 'maybe we'll have a glorious sunny day tomorrow. I think we deserve it, don't you? I imagine you miss the weather in France – am I right?'

'Yes, I do miss it now I'm over here. I miss it a lot. Look, Richard, if you fancy a break I'd be happy to drive for a while. We could leave the main road and find a pub first. Mind you I suspect some of the pubs I once knew around here will have closed long ago.'

'It's okay, Karen, I don't need a break from driving but the pub sounds a good idea.'

'No, Richard, seriously. I don't mind the dark and I first started my driving in this part of the world. Anyway as I haven't driven in the UK since I left for France, maybe I should get used to being on the wrong side of the road again. You've had things all your own way so far so be a good boy and do as you're told – but let's find the pub first.'

'Yes, Maam - if you say so, Maam,' he grinned looking down at the small screen, 'but there's nothing much indicated on the satnav so I don't expect we'll find anywhere other than the odd village for a few miles now we're up in them thaar hills. Look, by the time we do find somewhere it might leave us too late to carry on further. We could head for one of the larger villages. We could find ourselves a hotel or a pub with accommodation and decent food – oh, and the bottle of champagne I promised you.'

'Yes, let's do that,' said Karen, peering through the windscreen, 'and if it's a brighter day tomorrow I can drive and you can take in the scenery. You might be surprised how attractive the Peak District is even this late on in the year – in fact all year round as I remember it. And now the rain's stopped, the clouds are breaking up and I can see a lovely big moon.'

'Ah, did you see that!' he exclaimed, slowing the car, 'We just passed a turn off sign!'

Karen glanced aside. 'Sorry, Richard, I wasn't looking that way. What was on it?'

The car slowed further. 'Dunno, I couldn't make out the name – but it pointed off to the left so there must be a - yes - there's a turn-off just ahead of us.'

They steered off the highway soon to find themselves on a side road that quickly became a narrow, winding country lane bounded by overgrown hedges. Richard, slowed the car almost to a standstill and eyed the satnav closely. 'Damn, that wasn't such a good idea was it. From the looks of things we should have carried on a few miles further. It looks as if this road wanders through the hills to nowhere in particular then peters out.' Both peered down the lane ahead, illuminated by their headlights, as Richard added, 'In fact it's so full of potholes and weeds it's hardly a road at all. If there was a sign of any sort saying it was closed then it must have been overgrown and out of sight.'

'It might still be used by farm tractors,' offered Karen as the car began to move forward.

'Maybe,' he said, gazing through the windscreen into the obscurity beyond their lights. 'Well if it is I only hope none of 'em come along now though it doesn't look to me like anyone's used it in ages. I'll turn around and go back as soon as I can find enough space; there has to be somewhere along here. Hm, perhaps I should have chosen a smaller car.'

'No, Richard, this one's perfectly all right; I never feel comfortable in small cars. They're for small towns and villages.'

'Well I wouldn't mind a small town or even a village right now.' Further on they went until another turn-off appeared in the headlights to their left. 'That isn't showing on the screen at all,' he remarked. 'It must be private access of some sort.'

'Does that matter?' Karen asked. 'Shouldn't we turn around here in case there isn't anywhere further on?'

Richard slowed the car again to walking pace. 'Okay - yes, might be easier if I head into it and then back out.' He steered onto the rough surface of the lane, finding that it curved out of sight. 'Dammit,' he began, 'I don't think we should have - !'

'Oh god, I see what you mean,' she breathed, staring ahead.

On either side of their car and directly ahead, rising abruptly out of the darkness, the headlights revealed grassy embankments studded with angular rocks, some of which had slid down from both sides to restrict the width of the lane. Their wheels were crunching stones so Richard slowed to a standstill, saying, 'It doesn't look as if this is used any more – I doubt it goes anywhere other than a cow field - if they have cows in this part of the world.'

Twisting about to look over her shoulder, Karen asked. 'Can you back up? Surely we can't go any further down this.'

Richard stared into the rear-view mirror for a moment. 'No - can't see a bloody thing, it's pitch black and the rear hazard warning indicator's no help. It's too restricted with all that rubble for me to risk backing out without grinding against one of those rocks.'

'Then let me get out and guide you along,' offered Karen.

'Oh no you don't,' he responded, switching off the radio that had now become a distraction, 'you're not dressed for it and those nice shoes of yours would be ruined. Look, I'll go on a bit further; it must once have led somewhere worthwhile or it wouldn't be here. Hopefully it'll get wider or there'll be some place to manoeuvre not too far along; if there isn't then I'll get out and you can back the thing. My shoes won't suffer as much as yours.' With a broad smile he added, 'Anyway, you did offer to drive earlier.'

The car jolted and swayed but in less than a minute the lane was opening out. The beam of their headlights swept across to illuminate what appeared an area of waste-ground overgrown with scrub and weeds. Here and there arose low mounds of earth or gravel. Wide pools of dark water ripple-shattered reflections of a full moon that cast a waxen glow over the clearing.

'Christ, what a place to find ourselves in,' breathed Richard. 'It must be one of those areas where they used to store road building materials and stuff like that. It looks pretty dodgy either way and according to the satnav we're floating in the middle of nowhere. Now let me see, do I go all the way around it or do I risk staying closer to the middle?' He leaned closer to the windscreen then declared, 'I'll do a U-turn to our right closer to the middle - it seems level enough there.'

'At least now the sky's cleared we can see better,' said Karen as Richard steered the car about. 'Oh, there's another track leading off ahead but it's definitely not the one we came along.'

Richard peered hard into bleak darkness. 'No - absolutely not, I don't think anyone would want to go down there and neither do I. I'll carry on around.'

'Careful, Richard - it looks awful!'

The car rocked from side to side as they continued slowly across undulating ground and through shallow water. 'We're surrounded by so much rubble,' he muttered, 'I can hardly see where we came in.'

'There,' responded Karen, pointing into the night, 'I can see where we need to go – it's a bit further over to the right.'

'Ah, yes, that's the very one. Good - now we can get out of here the way we came in.'

The car shook and they continued along but then the sound of the engine rose dramatically and wet earth spattered beneath the front wheels. He pushed the gear stick into reverse and let out the clutch. The engine revved hard, rising and falling, the car swayed but would not move forward or backward. Further attempts achieved nothing more and Richard cursed aloud. Karen glanced at him anxiously as he let the gears into neutral and slumped back into the seat. 'Karen, love, the blasted car is stuck good and proper.'

A tense silence then she asked, 'Is there anything in the back we can jam under the wheels?'

'No, I've thought about that; there are only our personal things. I'll have to get out and look around for something to shove underneath, an old plank maybe. I can use my phone as a torch if I have to. At least the rain has gone. We'd better keep the engine running.'

Chill air invaded the car as Richard eased himself out. Soft grit gave way beneath his shoes as he looked across what struck him at once as a hostile realm of desolation. Away from the headlights the illumination from his phone was of less help than that of the full moon as he walked about, avoiding pooled water, seeing nothing he considered might be of use. There was no plank, no conveniently sized tree branch, just here and there a scattering of stones. Perhaps a few stones might be the answer so he set about to gather as many as he could carry, regretting as he did so that dirt would adhere to his hands and soil his clothes and the fact that his shoes must already be sullied. But his main regret was that he had begun a relationship with such promise, a relationship with the woman to whom he had offered much yet who had now been side-lined into what had to be the most regrettable of circumstances through a stupid error of judgement. His own. All hope of redemption might have depended upon his locating a piece of scrap wood but even that prospect seemed to be eluding him.

Watched intently by Karen he returned to the car and, in the glare of the headlights, stooped to ram a number of stones under each front wheel. She felt sorry for the man, knowing what he had to do, or try to do, while she sat waiting in relative comfort. Karen let down the side window and Richard, peering through it, asked her, 'Can you slide over into my seat?'

'Yes, all right – then what?'

'Okay, when you're ready, put her in second gear and try to get us moving while I shove as hard as I can from behind. Get ready for when I shout.'

'Yes!' she called as he moved away, 'I'll do that!'

He stepped to the rear of the car as Karen struggled across to position herself before the steering wheel where, confronted by a manual gearshift, she depressed the clutch, slipped the lever into second and gripped the wheel. Richard called, 'Okay let her go but easy does it!' as with outstretched arms he braced himself against the car. Karen revved the engine, letting out the clutch pedal slowly until it engaged. The wheels turned, Richard heaved, his shoes slithering on loose grit. The wheels began to spin, the car shuddered, lurched forward, then fell back. 'Try again!' he called but a second and third attempt, followed by a fourth from the front of the car, achieved nothing more. He reappeared at the side as Karen manoeuvred herself back into the passenger seat. He brush-slapped his hands one against the other, fell into the driver's seat then dutifully tapped his shoes together to dislodge the grit before drawing in his legs. 'It looks like we're dug in even deeper,' he sighed. 'I'll find our location on the satnav then I guess I'll have to call up the roadside assistance that came with the car hire. I have their paperwork in the glove compartment.'

Karen watched in silence as he selected the satnav options, heard him curse under his breath, then he exclaimed, 'Got it at last and it's showing our co-ordinates!' He withdrew the car hire papers then turned to her. 'Look, Karen, love, I'm really sorry I've got us into this mess. I'll make it up to you ten times over, I promise I will.'

Karen glanced at him but said nothing as Richard switched on his phone and began to finger-swipe the screen. He peered at it for tense seconds then, 'There's no signal,' he groaned. 'It's the latest model I have here and there's no bloody signal!'

'Let's give mine a try,' she said. Free of her safety belt Karen was able to twist about and retrieve her shoulder bag from the rear seat. 'It's an older one than yours but you never know.'

Richard watched her switch on and gaze down at her screen. Karen touched her screen, drew breath and said, 'No, I can't get anything either.'

'It must be this damned area,' he murmured angrily. 'It simply isn't covered because hardly any bugger lives here.'

'Yes,' she conceded, 'it must be away from any town or village and we're surrounded by hills. We'll have to walk all the way back to the main road, won't we? If there's still no signal there then we'll have to try and wave someone down.'

'I don't think we could rely on anyone stopping,' responded Richard, 'Would you at this time of the night? I don't think I would and I don't recall seeing any roadside phones. Anyway, the side road we turned off might not see any traffic until morning, if it ever does from the looks of it - and the main road has to be at very least a mile away.'

'Then what -?' she asked.

'The only thing I can think of right now is that I look around further for something to get us out of this. There were plenty of larger stones lying about on that track we came along. God, there has to be something -.'

Peering from her side window into the night, Karen exclaimed, 'Richard, switch off the headlights!'

'What?'

'The headlights - switch them off!'

A click, and a silent tide of darkness engulfed them. The clouds were almost entirely dissipated and the clearing became an eerie moonlit stage beneath a sweep of stars. 'What is it?' he asked.

'Richard I can see a light! There's a light over there, on the side opposite to where we came in. Can you see it? There must be a house further along that first track.'

'I can't see anything from here. Hang on - I'll get out.'

Chill air flooded once more into the car as the door swung open. Again outside, Richard opened the rear door and reached in to retrieve his jacket. For a while there was silence as he stepped around to the passenger side, then his face reappeared at the window. 'Yes, I can see the light. It's pretty dim but, as you say, I reckon that first track we spotted must lead to it.' Karen, too, eased herself from the car, gazed into the night and felt her high heels sink into soft grit as Richard said, 'If it's a farm, they'll have something to help get us out of here. You stay and keep the engine running so you don't get cold. I'll head off over there and get them to lend me a spade – that ought to do the job. They'll just have to understand we're in a damned awful mess.'

A moment's hesitation then Karen said, 'Richard, the light's disappeared.'

'Damn, they could be settling down to watch television. They'll be none too pleased to have a complete stranger banging on the door this time of the night.'

'We should both go,' said Karen. 'It will look better if there are two of us.'

'No, there's no point in getting your shoes ruined as well as mine is there,' he answered, pulling on and buttoning up his jacket. 'Better if you stay with the car. I think I figured out the general direction but it has to be somewhere close to that track in any case. I should be able to see well enough with the moon being out and our side lights will help me find my way back.'

'All right but - Richard, please be careful.'

'I'll be as careful as I can,' he assured her, backing away from the car, his form illuminated weakly by the sidelights.

Karen watched him move off, watched him glance cautiously about before receding into darkness. Then he was gone, a shadow engulfed by blackness. Returning to her seat, she waited with the window slightly down, listening. Apart from an occasional bluster of wind, there was only the reassuring sound of the car engine to mitigate encroaching night.

She had not considered how long he might be gone, nor had she thought to look at her watch or the dashboard clock as he left, though many minutes seemed to have passed. The sky remained clear, its dark vault possessed of only a few straggling clouds to keep meagre company with the moon and stars. Karen wondered if the clouds and the rain might return as quickly as they had departed. She hoped Richard would be back and the car freed before the weather closed in again. She switched on the radio and gazed out into darkness as the announcer stated it was time for the nine-o-clock news. She wondered also if, once back on the road, would they be able to find accommodation so late in the evening. Again she peered from the window, this time letting it down all the way to feel the night air bathe her face but still there was no sign of Richard. She imagined spectral forms just beyond her vision. Figures moving about in the shadows amidst those piles of rubble, eyes staring across at her, a lone figure cast adrift in a bubble of light. The interior of the car was becoming chilly so Karen turned the heating up and part closed the window.

The news had finished and with the engine still running the interior of the car was now much warmer. But Karen had become restless and impatient. 'Richard where are you?' she whispered. 'Where the hell *are* you?' The dashboard clock indicated almost nine-thirty. 'Something must be wrong,' she breathed. She switched off the radio and the engine. An avalanche of silence descended, an ominous quietness that served only to emphasise her isolation. She peered into the night, to the direction from which he should long since have reappeared. 'I can't just sit here like this,' she said aloud. 'Five minutes – five more minutes and I'll have to try and find out what's happened to him.'

The five minutes had barely elapsed when she reached into the rear seat to take hold of her coat. She would leave the safety and security of the car and enter the great night but she would not take the ignition keys. There was no point in her locking the car. She was outside, buttoning her coat against the chill and pulling on her shoulder bag as the high heels of her shoes sank further into wet ground. Hair fluttered against her cheek as she looked anxiously about. The night was all consuming, a sea of darkness that threatened to steal away her warmth and her soul.

Walking proved more difficult than Karen had anticipated. The light from her phone proved of less help than did the brightness of the moon. Twice she almost stumbled, twice she almost fell to her knees. There were the pools to be avoided. They could be deep - perhaps very deep. She was trying hard not to be afraid as she reached the downward sloping track but being so very alone she was beset by stirrings of elemental fear. She tugged her coat tighter. Often she looked back to the diminishing glow of the car lights but these vanished as she descended further. Eventually she was able to step aside from the mud and grit of the track to find wet grass under her feet. In the pallid light of the moon, she looked about, wondering if she might see his footprints but there was nothing to indicate anyone had passed that way. 'Richard,' she breathed, 'for god's sake where *are* you?'

She walked on further, treading warily, glancing repeatedly over her shoulder. Ahead she was able to make out vague forms, angular outlines against the sky. Yes - there was a building, perhaps several buildings, but there were no lights showing. Moonlight glinted from slate rooftops. She was aware of a farmyard odour, an odour of animals, and she recalled briefly the countryside riding school she once attended in her teens. She returned to the wide, sunken track that appeared to lead toward the buildings because she felt certain this was the route Richard would have taken. She continued on, cautious step by cautious step, to find the track firmer though much overgrown. 'Richard,' she gasped, 'where are you?' Then loudly, at the top of her voice, she called 'Richard, can you hear me! Richard – where are you!' but the breeze carried her words into infinite darkness.

Moving along the track and closer to the buildings, Karen stopped to call out again, 'Richard, where are you! Richard!' She glanced back in the direction she had taken, shivering through more than just the chill air. The car, had she been able to see it, must by this time be no more than a faint glimmer far out on a dark ocean. Was it possible Richard had returned there by a track she had missed? Might he now be peering about, calling her name, desperately worried over her absence? Or perhaps the night had deceived them both. Perhaps the light they had seen was not from this place but somewhere much further away and he had continued on to find it. Worse – could an accident have befallen him? After some moments thought, Karen did not believe Richard had returned to the car. No, had he called out she would surely have heard his voice carried on the night air. Nor did she believe he had gone any further than the vague cluster of buildings that arose before her. She wondered what to do next but was afraid to go on. She stepped back onto the grassy rise next to the track and turned once more to look across at the buildings. Before her, cast by moonlight, was her shadow. She looked down at the shadow then back to the buildings. Something moved. She looked again at her shadow. Now there were two shadows. Another had appeared beside her own - another, much larger shadow. Karen had no time to turn, no time to ask herself how she knew the shadow that loomed and merged with her own was not that of Richard. She was seized, taken in a grip of iron by hands far bigger and courser than his. She cried aloud, attempted to squirm about – attempted to see the face of her assailant. Something fell across her mouth - a suffocating hand of rough flesh that engulfed the lower part of her face. The other arm, lifting her from the ground, felt as if it might crush the life out of her as she kicked and struggled to get free. Twisting her head aside she glimpsed, for briefest of moments, a face. Had she not first passed out, Karen would have screamed.

Chapter 4

She was possessed by a nightmare. As she wormed upward from the deepest layers of oblivion an inner voice was telling her that's what it must be. A nightmare. Yet pirouetting briefly through Karen's mind were other images. The evening with Richard. The hotel room. Murmuring traffic and endless lights. Endless rivers of light that could go on forever. She was stirring to full consciousness but when she opened her eyes there was only darkness and she wondered if the nightmare might have been no dream at all. Once again she saw the face and could feel the unyielding grip of those arms about her. She wanted to cry out but held her breath then gasped aloud.

She was fully dressed and lay on her back, not on an ordinary bed but on a rough blanket under which she could feel and smell straw. An overpowering smell of straw, and from beyond it an odour of timber and cathedral-crypt stone. Her head was clearing, her senses becoming alert. She wanted to call for help and ask why and where she was. From beyond this shroud of dark bewilderment someone was calling her name. A hollow voice that seemed to echo from within a great cavern. She was aching, trembling with cold and fear but she knew the voice. She raised hands to her cheeks then remained still as she tried to comprehend what had, what was happening.

Again the voice, 'Karen, can you hear me? Karen, are you there?' His words echoed again through the darkness.

She reached out a hand, attempted to raise herself up but her hand pressed against rough concrete. 'Richard,' she called, 'w-where are we? I can't see anything.'

'Karen, are you all right? Are you hurt?'

'Hurt? I – I don't know, I don't think so. Richard, I can't see anything. Why is it so dark? Where are we?'

'Karen, it's pitch black in here and I can't see a damn thing either! Keep talking! Just keep talking and I'll find my way to you! You'll be okay!'

'Richard, where are we? Have we been in an accident?'

'No there was no accident.' His voice was very close. 'What happened to you? Can you remember?'

'Remember? Wait, I – yes, I remember, you went away. I left the car. I was trying to find you but – but there was someone else. Someone got hold of me and put a hand over my mouth. Oh, god it was awful! His face - it looked like a mask. A horrible mask!'

Richard was by her side and now his hand alighted on her shoulder. 'Okay, love, I'm here.'

'Richard,' she asked again as she grasped his arm, 'where are we?'

'It's some kind of barn or stable and I think we're locked in. Karen, did you see them? Did anyone say anything to you?'

'Say anything? Who? What d'you mean? It was only what I said – that hideous man, and he didn't say anything. Please, Richard – why can't you tell me what's happening? Why are we here in the dark?' She reached about with her free hand, fingers touching only the blanket, the thick layer of straw then the cold floor.

'Right - remember when I left you?'

'Yes I remember, of course I do. I waited in the car for a long time. I waited for ages but you didn't come back so I tried to find you; I followed the way you went. Why didn't you come back?'

'Karen, I walked down the track toward where I thought we'd spotted the light but all I could see was the outline of some buildings. I went closer to check if there was any sign of life. I thought maybe the main house would be obvious but I couldn't tell what was what, even with a full moon so I looked about to see if I could find anything to help us get the car out. I came across a few planks propped up by a wall so I decided to take one rather than try to find anybody. I didn't want any complications – I just wanted to get back to you and the car. That was okay so I thought, and I – yes, I remember I'd walked a few yards and I know I'd got as far as the track. I remember hoping I'd soon get to see our car lights in the distance and then I'd be able to concentrate on those because the moon was hidden behind a cloud and I could hardly see where I was going. Then I caught my foot in something - a sheet of corrugated iron I think. It sounded like a thunderclap when the plank hit it and I went sprawling. That's when the damned honking started.

91

It must have been the noise I made. Geese, I think - and it sounded like they were somewhere over the other side of the buildings. For a minute or so I couldn't get up. I just lay there wondering if I'd broken any bones. I managed to get to my feet and picked up the plank but I'd only gone a few steps when someone grabbed me from behind and knocked me senseless. I didn't hear or see the bastard but it felt like somebody big and very powerful. Next thing I remember is lying flat out in the dark and hearing a door close and a bar being slid across the outside. I got up intending to walk around but I couldn't see a damned thing. That must have been after they'd brought you in but I didn't realise anyone else was here until I heard you moaning.'

'Are you hurt?' she asked, squeezing his hand.

'Nothing too serious as far as I know,' he replied. 'I twisted my arm a bit when I fell and the side of my face is pretty tender. I don't know if I hit my head when I went down but I do know he whacked me. I dare say my suit is pretty well messed up but apart from that -.'

'Richard, I tried to find you. I got to the farm and shouted. He or they must have heard me. Who are they? Why have they done this to us? Why are we locked in here? Do they think we were thieves?'

'Thieves, us?' he answered. 'No, it might be the other way around. It could be we've come across something they don't want the outside world to know about. If they thought we were thieves, they'd have had the police here by now. If only.'

'You mean it might be a criminal gang of some sort?'

'Yes, that's what I'm thinking. Stolen property, drug dealers, a bunch of bloody terrorists - I don't know. What I do know is that we need to find a way out of here. Can you stand up okay? Come on, I'll help you.'

'I think so,' replied Karen, placing a hand on his shoulder as she struggled to her feet. 'God, I'm cold and I ache everywhere. I only hope I can walk.'

'You have to,' said Richard, taking her hand in his. 'We need to get out of here, like now.'

'How do we get out? You said someone locked us in.'

'Maybe they did but we can't sit around waiting. We'll feel our way along the wall and keep on turning left until we find something. Maybe there'll be another door. We have to try.'

'Richard, can't we use the light from your phone?'

'I left the damned thing in the car,' he replied. 'What about yours?'

'It – it was in my shoulder bag but I don't know where that is. Is your watch luminous? Can you see the time?'

'Yes, just about - it's - it's getting on for ten-thirty.'

'I can hear the wind outside.' Karen said. 'Can you hear it?'

'Yes, it must be coming through somewhere. Maybe it's getting in under the roof.'

'There are two windows,' she said, gazing upward. 'They look fairly small but I can just see the stars outside.'

'I looked at those windows as well but they're too high up even if we could get through, which I doubt.' He reached to the wall and placed a right hand against cold stone. They stepped cautiously forward, each with a right hand feeling tentatively along the rough surface, Karen's left-hand clutching Richard's jacket. 'Be careful,' he said. 'Careful you don't trip over anything and keep close to me.'

'I wasn't about to wander off on my own, Richard, I promise you.' Then a thump was followed by 'Oh, Christ!'

'Richard – what happened?'

'I nearly went flying over something. Wait, I – I can feel what it is. I think - yes it's my small case - yes it definitely is my case but I can't see a blasted thing so there isn't any point in my opening it. Whoever it was banged us up in here must have gone out to the car as well.'

'Is there anything in your case that might help us?' she asked.

'Nothing I can think of, no. All I packed was the usual stuff for two or three days away; a change of clothes, electric shaver, toiletries, that sort of thing. I'll prop it up against the wall.'

Several steps further and they found themselves at an abrupt left turn. They carried on unspeaking until Richard faltered and exclaimed, 'Oh, hell, what's this?'

'What, Richard - what is it?'

'Feels like a stack of straw. We'll work our way around it, okay. Are you still all right?'

'As right as I can be under the circumstances,' she murmured, almost stumbling as she sought to keep a hold on his jacket.

They negotiated bales of straw, reached another corner, a second left turn and carried on a short way then Richard said, 'Ah, here's a - it feels like a wooden partition. We'll have to make our way around it. Maybe we'll come across a spade, a rake or something I can use to try and get us out of here.'

'It could be a stall for animals,' said Karen as they groped their way around and back along the wooden barrier. 'There can't be any animals in here though, we'd have smelled or heard them if there were.'

'I guess you're right,' he muttered. 'Barging into a horse or a blasted cow isn't my idea of fun at the moment. Ah, I'm back at the wall and it's solid stone again. We won't be getting out through there in a hurry, that's for sure.'

'It would have to be a stone building to keep people inside, wouldn't it – if that's what they wanted. What now?'

'We have to keep going,' he answered, finding another partition blocking their path.

The decision to carry on around this next obstruction brought them back to the wall then eventually to another abrupt left turn. Moments later they reached the stable doors. Richard heaved against creaking timbers; they heard the bar outside grate and rattle but the doors would not give.

'The damn things are much too solid for anyone to force open,' he breathed. 'I can just about see through the gap but I can't make out anything in the dark. There are no lights – nothing.' Close to the gap he called, 'Hey, let us out of here!' Then again, this time banging on the doors. 'Is anyone there? Let us out of here!'

They waited. They listened for voices, for approaching footsteps. Richard called again, and again they waited. There was no response. At first the only sound from beyond the doors was of a breeze that sighed coolly through the gap. But the breeze was increasing in strength and soon they became aware of another sound.

'Can you hear that?' Richard asked.

Karen moved closer and listened. 'It sounds like a dog or some animal wailing?'

'A dog? No, I don't think that's a dog. It sounds more like voices – like some kind of - like a distant chorus. I don't think it's their television.'

They listened a while longer then Richard called out yet again, thumping as hard as he was able then kicking against the doors. 'No use is it,' he breathed, 'if they're in that house with the television on they won't hear a damned thing.'

'God,' exclaimed Karen, 'they can't leave us locked in here like this! They just can't!'

'Yes, well that's exactly what they have done and I've a feeling they may not be coming back for some time - maybe not until morning.'

'Oh, no,' Karen sighed, 'why d'you say that?'

'Those blankets and straw beds. I don't suppose they'd be in here otherwise.'

'It's almost as if they'd been expecting us,' she said, 'but that's impossible.'

'You're right, that's impossible,' he murmured, 'the straw beds must have been in here already. So – so all we can do is keep going until we end up where we started out.'

'Then what?' she asked.

'Then what,' Richard sighed, 'Karen, love, I only wish I knew.'

They continued on past the doors - probing, feeling only rough stone, knowing only each other's breathing and presence, finding no means of escape and no implement that might be of service. When his foot kicked against straw, Richard said, 'We're back to where we were, I'm sure of it.'

'Yes, we are, I can feel one of the blankets. Richard, what d'you think is the reason -? No, it's a stupid question isn't it. It doesn't matter what either of us thinks, does it. We're prisoners here until they, whoever they are, decide to let us out.'

'I can't stand around and do nothing,' he said. 'I'll have another go at those doors. Maybe something will give.'

'It's no use is it, Richard. We both know that. It's like you said, the doors are too solid.'

A dozen heartbeats passed before he spoke again. 'Yes - okay, it looks like there's nothing we can do until someone shows up. In that case we'd better get under the blankets to rest a while. Let's see if I can shift one of these layers of straw closer so we can talk and try to keep warm. I'm feeling the cold so I know you must be.'

'Yes, it seems colder in here than it was out there,' answered Karen sitting down and pulling the heavy woollen cover over herself. Richard, searching about in darkness, was eventually able to slide the other straw mattress and blanket closer to Karen's rough bed. 'At least I still have my raincoat,' she said. 'They must have taken my shoulder bag with all my personal things. I had all my money and my cards in that shoulder bag. I wonder if that's what they're after. They probably have my holdall as well.'

'I don't think it's money they're after,' he said after some hesitation, 'I still have my wallet here. I can feel my cash and my cards are still in it; they could easily have helped 'emselves to those.'

'Then what is it they want with us?' Karen sighed.

'I dare say we'll find out sooner or later,' he answered.

In the darkness they shuffled nearer to each other and their hands joined.

For a time there was silence, then, 'Oh, Richard,' she whispered, 'what have we got ourselves in to?'

***

'Karen,' he breathed, leaning close to her. 'Karen, love, can you hear me? Karen, wake up.'

Karen stirred and sighed, 'Oh, god where am I? I remember something awful. What's happening? Where are we?'

Grey morning light filtered through the pair of small windows high in the wall opposite to where they had spent a night of troubled, intermittent sleep. There was by then enough light for them to better ascertain the nature of the space to which they had been confined. Richard clambered to his feet and Karen sat up, glancing about to see if her shoulder bag had lain unseen nearby. It had not. Richard peered at his watch: it indicated twenty-five minutes past six. They stared about the stable then Richard helped her to her feet. Each assessed the appearance of the other and Karen, raising a hand part way to his cheek, said, 'Oh, your face is bruised down one side.'

'I can feel it burning' he breathed, lifting a hand to tender skin. 'At least you seem to be intact.'

Both were dishevelled and Richard, slipping off his already loosened tie, peered down at his mud-stained clothes and shoes to exclaim, 'Look at my damned suit – ruined!'

'And my shoes,' remarked Karen, easing on her high heels, 'but I think messed-up clothes are the least of our problems.'

Pulling a tissue from her pocket, Karen wiped the old mascara from her eyes and smoothed down her unkempt hair, asking, 'Have you heard anything or anyone – anything at all?'

'No, nothing except cows, clucking hens and those bloody geese that gave me away.'

'They have to let us out of this awful place soon, Richard. They have to.'

'Yes, and then we'll need a damned good explanation from them – and compensation. I wonder what our company lawyers will have to say about kidnapping and assault – if they deal with that kind of thing.'

'Perhaps,' she continued, glancing at the doors, 'perhaps it was – yes, it must have been some kind of misunderstanding. Surely it must.'

'Misunderstanding? I hope so. Maybe they really did think we were trying to steal from them. I suppose people steal from farms the way they do from anywhere else but like I said, they would have called the police, wouldn't they. No, there has to be more to it than that. We can do nothing but wait until one of 'em shows up.'

Richard bent to open his small suitcase and Karen said, 'At least you've got your case. I don't have anything of mine.

'They've been through my case,' he said. 'Looks like they've tipped everything out, my change of clothes and other things, then just stuffed it all back in.'

'Is there anything missing?' she asked.

'It's difficult to tell, especially in this light. Nothing I can say for sure but there was nothing of much value in there to start with except maybe a few company papers and they're still in here.' He refastened and picked up the case then they walked slowly about the stable, seeing the piled up bales of straw and the empty wooden stalls they had earlier negotiated in total darkness and again looking up to confirm how small and beyond reach were the windows. The windows revealed only grey sky. It was obvious also that there was no other door and except for the blankets, the straw bedding and the bales of straw at the far end, the building was empty.

100

Richard had glanced again at his watch to see the time was almost seven o'clock when there were sounds from beyond the stable doors. A woman's voice - then footsteps getting closer. Richard and Karen moved toward the doors and halted a few steps away. A sudden metallic rattling. The growling of an iron bar being drawn aside. The doors shuddered and rumbled. A split of daylight appeared and grew wider as one of the pair of doors slowly opened. A figure stood silhouetted against grey morning light – the slight figure of a woman holding a levelled shotgun.

Richard eyed the gun, stepped forward and demanded, 'What the hell is going on here - out with it - and why are you pointing that thing at us?'

'Please,' asked Karen, 'Why have you done this to us?'

The woman remained silent but glared at them with harsh blue eyes grotesquely enlarged behind thick spectacle lenses. Her tight-curled grey hair, long floral cotton dress with wide collar and her green cotton pinafore might under different circumstances have given rise to humorous comment.

'Come on then!' Richard pressed, angrily, 'Just *what* is going on here? What's all this about?' He ventured another step forward but a second figure moved into sight and though silhouetted against the sky, Karen recognised the face, clasped hands to her cheeks and cried out, 'Oh - oh god! Richard, it's him!'

Eyes now adjusted to the morning light, Richard and Karen beheld a brute of a man in the rugged attire of an outdoor labourer, his twisted face hideously disfigured and discoloured by a lurid gash running down the left side of his head from above his eye to his jaw. A gash that in healing had distorted his mouth into a snarling grin, a grin that had left a part of his jaw exposed to reveal shattered teeth as he attempted a grotesque smile. Karen's nightmare stood before them!

'Do nowt and stay exactly as you are,' the woman ordered. 'Try anythin' foolish and Grimshaw will break yon lad like a dry stick!'

'What d'you want with us?' Richard demanded, holding out his hands. 'What's the point in all this?'

'The point?' she responded, raising the shotgun higher. 'The point is my prayers 'ave been answered by 'im above and that's all that matters. Aye, you'll see soon enough.'

'See what!' cried Karen. 'What has anything around here got to do with us? Why are we -?'

'Now look!' cut in Richard, 'whatever you think, all we wanted to do was get our car back onto the road! We came to get help and nothing else. What's wrong with that?'

'What's wrong with that?' the woman repeated, stepping back. 'Matter is you were sent 'ere like I said - so out you both come. The girl first.'

Richard and Karen eyed each other and Richard declared, 'I've no idea what you're talking about. Nobody's sent us from anywhere so point that damned gun away and let us leave right now!'

The woman turned again to her menacing companion. 'Grimshaw, get 'er out first.'

'Aye, Ma,' the man growled. 'Get 'er out first.'

Grimshaw, for that was how the woman had referred to him, stepped into the stable. Richard looked about in desperate hope of seeing something to use as a weapon, some object they might earlier have missed – a metal implement, a rock, anything. But the woman now had her shotgun pointed directly at him. Would she use it? Could he take that chance?

Karen backed away, clutching instinctively at her coat, but the bear-like Grimshaw darted forward, less like a bear, more like a big cat, to seize her arm. Richard let fall his case and moved quickly to intervene. He attempted to push Karen's assailant away but Grimshaw struck him a blow on the jaw that sent him tumbling to the floor. Karen screamed, 'Richard!' She struggled frantically to free herself as she was dragged from the stable into cold morning air. The woman moved to shut the stable door and Karen, twisting about as the door closed, caught a glimpse of Richard clambering to his feet with a hand pressed to the side of his face. 'Let me go!' she yelled, 'Get your bloody hands off me!' but her plea was ignored.

The woman, her shotgun lowered, joined them to stand, appearing diminutive, by the side of her menacing companion to whom she said, 'Now, lad, take this one to the 'ouse and we'll leave 'er man in there 'till later.'

Karen offered only token resistance, aware she had no chance of freeing herself from his grip and saying nothing as Grimshaw forced her along. Only then did she notice – spread across the back of his jacket in bold yellow letters, the word, Grimshaw.

She looked frantically about in the hope of seeing someone to whom she might call for help. Approaching the farmhouse, she spotted a semi-derelict vehicle at the front and the farm track that lead away to the clearing and eventually to the main road. Karen realised she had missed much of the track that previous night when treading rougher ground. They reached the porch at the front of the house and there the door stood ajar. The woman stepped inside and, having hesitated to unload the cartridges, which she dropped into the pocket of her apron, she propped the gun close by the door and gestured for Karen to follow. Grimshaw, though having released her arm, stooped low, blocking out light from the doorway as he entered the house behind her. There they halted and as she stood dismayed Karen felt a hand pass over her hair.

She spun about and cried out once again, 'Get your bloody hands off me!' almost stumbling as she attempted to back away.

'Now behave thaself, lad,' ordered the woman and Grimshaw drew back with that same hideous grin Karen had observed at the stable.

'Ahhh - p-pretty lady,' came a soft growl as Karen turned away from him. Trying hard to compose herself though possessed by fear unlike any she had known, she stared about the room. Other than for its beamed ceiling, it reminded her vaguely of the lounge at her parents' house though it might have belonged to a yet earlier generation. In those first brief moments she noted the small table set out with dishes and food for two people and the log fire blazing brightly at the far end. From the corner of her eye she noted also an old-fashioned telephone to the left of the main window. She wanted to rush for the phone and call for help but knew she would be seized before that happened.

'Sit thaself down at table,' the woman ordered. 'There's food and drink. You'll be needin' it.'

Karen glared hard at her. 'Food! What are you talking about? You've detained us against our will, that – that man of yours has assaulted Richard and you've threatened both our lives! What you have done is criminal! Don't you understand? When the police find out you'll be arrested and locked away - and find out they surely will!'

The woman's expression hardened further, her voice was a muted growl. 'Police. Law. There's only one law 'ereabouts and that is God's law.' Her voice rose higher as she went on, 'His voice is in the wind and you will 'ear it – yes, you will 'ear the Almighty speak as do I and then you will know!'

Karen glanced about to observe the hulk of the man she called Grimshaw waiting silently inside the doorway, his head bowed clear of the ceiling beams, the warped grin still set upon his mutilated face, his gaze fixed hard upon her. A thin streak of saliva glistened at one corner of his mouth as the grin transformed again into the bizarre parody of a smile. She turned, wide-eyed, to confront the woman once more. 'You're mad!' she declared. 'Y-you could be put away for years. Look, let us go and we'll say nothing, all right? We'll be on our way and forget all about this, I promise. We've got nothing - nothing whatsoever to do with you or with this place. Just – just let both of us go!'

'This is providence,' the woman replied softly, glancing briefly upward. Then her voice hardened as she declared, 'You were meant to be 'ere. Oh, I knew all along my prayers would be answered. So now you must do as I say and if you do not then – then the Lord's guidance must be followed, aye, as always it must be followed. You will 'elp in our day to day tasks and if either of you tries to leave then Grimshaw 'ere knows what to do.' She looked past Karen to the figure by the door and added, 'You know what to do if they causes us problems, don't you, lad?'

In a voice of stone grating hard upon stone he replied, 'I knock the m-man down, Ma. I m-make 'im not m-move anymore.'

'Good lad,' said the woman. 'Now you go an' wait outside until I calls you.'

Karen stared at her in mute disbelief as the ogre, for in her mind that was what he had become, stooped through and pulled shut the front door. Moments later the room darkened slightly and Karen realised he must be standing at the window, perhaps staring at her through the glass. 'All right,' she agreed, 'I'll sit down. I'll sit down if you'll tell me just what is going on.'

'Aye, sit and I'll sit also. As you see, girl, there's milk, cheese and bread ont' table. Good honest food from this farm. There'll be eggs, meat an' potatoes later int' day.'

Karen drew back the old, rustic chair and sat. The woman did likewise and now they faced one another over the table. Karen looked at the other's hands – hands that in her mind resembled much enlarged chickens' feet. 'We'll eat and drink now,' the woman said, 'then we'll talk and you will begin to understand - aye, that you will.'

Ignoring her words for the moment, Karen glanced at the food and the glass of milk. There was metal cutlery on the table, a fork and a knife - a sharp knife. She thought hard about the knife. Wild thoughts. Her hand was close enough. The woman was perhaps not as frail as she looked but it ought not to be difficult. Then what? What if she used the knife on her? There was the deformed man, the ogre, waiting for her call. He was obviously retarded. If he was watching from outside he might respond by re-entering the house, by attacking, perhaps killing her and then Richard.

'No, *you* understand,' Karen declared at last. 'I don't want food, I – we, don't want anything at all from you; I only want to know what this is all about and for you to agree that we leave here.'

'Eat then we'll talk,' the woman repeated, blandly. 'Until then I'll say nowt else.'

Karen considered the woman's words and in tense silence she stared down at the table. She could refuse to listen but it now occurred that agreeing to some form of explanation might lead to her and Richard being allowed their freedom. She picked up the glass and sipped cautiously. The milk was tepid. It tasted different less pleasant than the pre-packaged, heat-treated milk she knew. The wood fire punctuated their silence with an occasional hiss and crack. Karen now regretted her acceptance of the milk because it might be taken as a concession to the woman's demands.

107

'You'll need to wash 'an all that int' back and change upstairs,' the woman said at last.

Karen stared at her, exclaiming angrily, 'What! What are you talking about?'

'Aye,' the woman continued as if Karen had said nothing, 'them city clothes and fancy shoes'll be no use to you out 'ere. Woodstove gets the water 'ot and cooks food just as it were meant to int' old days. You can wash y'self and other things an' there's toilet int' utility right past the kitchen.'

'Stop it!' cried Karen slamming down the less than a quarter empty glass.

'I'll 'ave Grimshaw bring your man friend over in good time. What's the man's name – Richard is it? Did I 'ear you call 'im Richard? D'you keep 'is picture in that locket or is it someone else?'

'Just – just never mind the locket!' Karen responded. 'You said you'd tell me what this is all about. I'll listen then you can let us both go – all right!'

'Suit y'self,' shrugged the woman, picking up a knife to slice for herself a piece of cheese, then another that she let lie there. 'And y'name, girl – what is it?'

'My name has got nothing to do with you!' retorted Karen, angrily. 'Nothing at all!'

'Well,' added the woman, it'll make things easier if I know it.'

'All right - it's Karen,' she answered coldly as she took up a slice of bread and the spare portion of cheese. She was hungry and if she refused further to accept food then the woman might call back in the figure hovering by the window. '*Now* will you tell me what's going on then let us leave?'

'I'm Elsie,' came the reply; 'Elsie Baxendale.' Peering down at Karen's left hand to see there was no wedding ring on her finger she added, 'I take it that man's not your 'usband.'

'No he isn't my husband; he's a business partner and that's all I'm telling you.'

'And I see you were both off somewhere together. An' where might that 'ave been?'

'Look, that's none of your business!' Karen responded. 'Now, please, can we end this nonsense?'

'Well it may not be my business but what folks get up to is the Lord's business. The good book tells us, "God will judge the adulterer and all the sexually immoral." Now I'd say a girl with your looks - a girl that dresses like you, must 'ave many male admirers. Aye, the temptations of the flesh are all too common in this world. So I think p'raps you 'ave a picture of a different man in that locket.'

Karen, having already spotted the large black Bible with metal clasps and gilded page edges laying by the old radio, glared at her and, half rising from the chair, exclaimed, 'How *dare* you preach morality to me after what you and that beast of a man have done to us! How *dare* you! Just when is this going to end?' She looked again at the knife, glanced aside to see that Grimshaw was, as she feared, staring through the window, then she fell back into the chair.

Mrs Baxendale seemed to read her thoughts and spoke almost casually, as if Karen's last remark had passed by her as no more than a gentle breeze. 'I suppose I 'ave to explain about the big lad an' why 'e's with me now.'

'No you don't have to explain anything at all,' responded Karen. 'I'm not in the least bit interested, so -.'

'Aye, maybe you are not,' cut in Mrs Baxendale, 'but it's a tale I 'ave to tell sooner or later and sooner is best.'

'So he isn't -.' began Karen. It had occurred to her in those passing moments that there might be some advantage to be gained if she was to discover more about who these people really were. Already she was thinking how she and Richard would report this bizarre episode to the police.

'He's not my son – I never 'ad no son, nor's the poor lad my 'usband. I don't know the lad's real name and neither does 'e. I call 'im Grimshaw because that's the name you'll 'ave maybe seen on't back of 'is jacket so Grimshaw it 'as to be. No, my Len, God bless 'im, joined 'is maker a good while back but with the Lord's 'elp I keep our work alive as he would 'ave wished.'

Karen stared at her, wondering if the woman would continue talking, wondering if she herself ought to prompt for more information or if she ought to further insist upon re-joining Richard and both being allowed to leave. She imagined Richard pacing up and down in the stable and desperately anxious to know what had happened to her.

'You'll 'elp inside this 'ous and your man will 'elp with tasks around the farm,' Mrs Baxendale

110

announced, 'because it's all too much for me ant' lad.'

'This is ridiculous!' exclaimed Karen, half rising once again from the chair. 'We're not going to help you with anything! Can't you see that?'

'We've no electricity now the generator's broke, no light except oil lamps an' candles and no water fromt' taps,' continued Mrs Baxendale. 'Aye, only good water for this 'ouse is fromt' old pump by the kitchen sink but that works well enough.'

Karen lowered back into the chair, shaking her head in disbelief at what was being implied. 'Now listen to me,' she insisted, leaning forward, 'Richard and I have *no* knowledge of farms, none whatsoever. He is an accountant and I am a secretary. We're of no use to you. No use at all – can't you see that.'

Mrs Baxendale also leaned forward and stared hard at her with cold, lens-distorted gaze, saying almost under her breath, 'Oh, one of *them* you say - a ruddy office-bound pen pusher like them that wanted to take away what were always Len's and mine by right. Well now, the Lord's will 'as become clearer than ever.'

'Richard hasn't taken anything away from anyone,' Karen insisted. 'Why d'you say that?'

'I'll tell you why like I said so better I do it now - aye I'll tell you now instead of later and your man can stay out there a while longer while you sits where you are an' listens.'

Karen glanced again at the window but Grimshaw was still there, now with his broad back to the glass and his given name displayed

111

intimidatingly large. Karen sat in anguished silence as the woman drank back her own glass of milk with infuriating gulps and began, 'This farm were in our family for generations past. Aye an' it were a good farm. When that big road were to be built all them years ago we cut back ont' livestock and let a good portion of our land out to them that needed it for quarryin' limestone. That went on for years and provided us with a good income. Aye, it were good money.

When they'd 'ad all the stone they wanted they walked off leavin' us with a big 'ole int' ground. Aye, but we'd got plenty money out of 'em so Len and I carried on wit' farm because it were all the life we knew. We were sellin' what surplus we 'ad at the nearest village market until that were shut down. Then later on we starts gettin' official letters and this man fromt' council comes along to tell us the access road were to be closed because the disused quarry made it too dangerous, an' as other farms were closin' down all't local services were bein' cut t'save money. They told us we'd 'ave to move away because there'd be no road maintenance. Aye, we would 'ave to go or we'd see our land cut off from't rest of the world.'

Mrs Baxendale helped herself casually to another portion of bread and cheese then continued, 'In the end we told the pen pushers we'd sell what livestock we 'ad left and we gave 'em a new address. Oh, but we'd 'eard God's message through the winds. Well before the movin' date we bought in all sorts of things we'd need for years ahead an' left it 'idden down int' quarry with fodder there and in't stable for some of our livestock. Then that were it – we left in case they came back to spy on us. They wanted no more of us by then so we returned soon after to reclaim what were ours. There were logs from the ash trees my Len 'ad cut an' stored so there were always wood fort' stove and fire. We 'ad a well-stocked green'ouse, the two cows, a few sheep, 'ens and geese so we'd enough to get by with a bit of 'ard work and my Len enlarged the vegetable plot. There were only one problem. We'd a generator for electric power and always 'ad to rely on that for lights, fort' wireless and much else. Well there were and maybe still is a works maintenance depot just a few miles up from 'ere but away from the main road so they weren't too bothered over security. Len knew all the old tracks 'ereabout so took 'is motorbike and trailer over an' 'elped 'imself whenever to extra stuff we'd not 'ad enough time to get earlier. Often he'd bring back a few extras like tea and coffee and made sure we'd plenty of paraffin stored up in case the depot closed.'

Mrs Baxendale had become so engrossed in her account that Karen, although seething with anger and impatience, feared the woman might react aggressively if interrupted and that Grimshaw, peering again through the window, still might re-enter the house.

'But,' continued Mrs Baxendale, 'they must 'ave wondered where't paraffin and such were goin' an' so left a man there to watch over it. Aye, it 'ad to 'appen sooner or later though for a time they must 'ave thought someone were gettin' in from't main road. That were well over a year ago. Len 'ad been over there one night and returned by mornin' but soon after, this big lad arrived fromt' depot to confront us while we were workin' int' garden. Aye, the man 'ad followed my Len back 'ere an' said he were goin' to report us to the police. But Len and I knew that we 'ad to follow the guidance from above or we'd sacrifice our 'ome and all we'd worked for. Len confronted 'im and told the man 'e must say nothin' as we were doin' no 'arm to no one an' just wanted to be left alone. We even offered to give back whatever we could but the man were 'avin' none of it. It were no good, no, 'e wouldn't listen an' started to push my Len about because 'e were right strong and Len stood in 'is way. I took 'old of a garden spade and passed it to Len while I grabbed the man's coat at the back. The man would 'ave knocked me an' my 'usband down and walked off to tell on us but Len raised the spade and struck 'im right 'ard with it. Aye, struck 'im 'ard as he possibly could. You see, we 'ad to stop 'im tellin' tales. Well the big lad went down and I thought, seein' all that blood and the great gash down the side of 'is 'ead, that he were done fer. My Len turned to me, gaspin' as I thought from exertion. Then he dropped the spade, clutched at 'is chest an' fell to the ground as well. His heart – it were never very strong. The effort 'ad been too much and I knew as I stood there that 'e were departed from this life, God rest his soul. No, 'e were not a fit man in those later years. It were me that carried most of the burden as nowadays I do more than ever.'

'So your husband murdered the workman,' breathed Karen. 'And you helped him. You murdered an innocent man for trying to do his job and now you propose to force other people, us, to help you out.' Almost at once she regretted her comment though Mrs Baxendale expressed no reaction.

'I 'ad to plan what best to do,' she continued, her eyes for the moment closed, her head lowered slightly, 'but as I stood there alone an' wonderin' 'ow to cope, the big man began to stir. He weren't dead though it looked as if 'e soon might be. But then I understood; I 'eard the Lord's voice once more on't wind. Yes, I knew then what I 'ad to do.'

Karen looked aside to the front door, muttering under her breath, 'We've got to get away from this mad old bitch. Richard, can you not get out of there? Please.'

Mrs Baxendale continued her tale, staring past Karen, eyes ablaze. 'Don't know 'ow I did it but with 'elp from above I got the lad to 'is feet and into the 'ouse. His face were split down one side – aye, split to the bone with some of 'is teeth gone. I some'ow got 'im int' kitchen and dressed the wound as best I could, still thinkin' he'd not last out the day but - but bless the Lord, 'e did. For weeks I nursed 'im and for weeks I 'ardly slept because the animals needed seein' to as well. I worked like I'd never worked before but the Almighty spoke and gave me strength to carry on. When the poor lad recovered 'e didn't know who 'e was. No, didn't remember nothin', not even 'is own name. He were a gift from above, see, because my Len 'ad passed on, so I took all the stuff out of the poor lad's pockets and burned it all in case 'e looked at it an' remembered who 'e was an' what my Len 'ad done. But 'e remembers nowt of the past and never will. After a while he called me, Ma, like he must 'ave called 'is own mother.'

'I take it no one ever bothered to come here looking for him,' Karen said, dryly.

'No they did not - never. And that were providence.' Karen noted the expression of stern satisfaction that set across the woman's face. 'He does work about the farm, simple work, liftin' 'eavy things, choppin' wood for the stove, muckin' out cows an' all that. He can't think too much for 'isself - no, just does what 'es told like a well-be'aved child though I've to be there some of the time in case the poor lad forgets what 'e's about.'

Karen continued to regard her and murmured, 'A retard with the mind of a child or an insane killer depending on what you tell him to do.' She wondered momentarily how Mrs Baxendale had disposed of her husband's body but was not about to ask.

'You'll understand soon enough,' she went on, 'you and your fancy man. You'll understand fully what it all means and why it's all 'appened this way. But now I've said all there is to say ont' subject go an' do your necessaries in't utility out the back. There's 'ot water ont' stove for washin' and you'll see a towel 'angin' up by the sink. Get yourself sorted then get upstairs – first room ont' left when y'turn onto the landing. That'll be yours from now on. There's sensible clothes int' cupboard - mine

116

from when I were younger. I were about your size in them days, aye, so 'appen they'll fit you well enough. While you're up there Grimshaw and I will fetch your fancy man in fromt' stable. He can do 'is necessaries, take 'is food then change into some of Len's old work clothes. There's plenty around 'ere needs to be done – aye, there's plenty, needs fixin' not least the generator.'

Karen arose abruptly from her seat, causing it almost to fall back. She was thinking once more to insist, to demand that she and Richard be allowed to leave, then she looked aside to see Grimshaw again staring through the window. His nail-head eyes were fixed firmly upon her and saliva glinted on his twisted jaw. She turned to Mrs Baxendale open-mouthed as the woman said, 'Never you mind our Grimshaw, 'e'll soon be elsewhere. You just find your way out the back an' get on with it. An' if you're still down 'ere when we get back with your man an' don't do as I say then, 'appen you'll both 'ave the lad to deal with.'

Yes, the "necessaries," as Mrs Baxendale had put it. Karen was fully aware of what was meant by the word and, after a night of confinement in the stable, the need to make use of whatever lay waiting was pressing her now to a degree she could no longer ignore. Without speaking, she stepped around the table and to the hallway opposite the window outside which Grimshaw loomed. And though she dared not look behind she knew his eyes remained upon her and fear prickled her flesh. The door was wide open so she entered the dim passage where a narrow flight of stairs ascended from her right into upper gloom. Moving cautiously to pull open the next door with trembling hand, Karen was confronted by the kitchen. Here was light from outside so she closed the door while not caring to look directly at the small window. Now for a time in isolation she beheld a room with high ceiling, a room dominated by an ornate, black-lacquered, steel woodstove; relic of another age. It contained an oven beside which was an iron grate where the fire glowed and high above this was fixed a drying rack for dishes. Copious heat from the wood stove charged the entire room. On the hot surface rested a large copper pan filled with simmering water and by it a smaller, empty pan. Immediately beyond the stove was an equally ancient, once white, cracked porcelain sink beside which arose an ornate iron water pump complete with curved lever. Above the sink was fixed a wooden shelf upon which Karen noted among other items, a bar of white soap resting in a small dish. Through a third doorway she entered what proved to be the utility room where stood a defunct fridge, washing machine and, positioned before them, an old iron mangle with wooden rollers. Ahead was the stout, curtain-covered outer door. On opening a door immediately to her right, she was confronted by the odour of a claustrophobic, dark and distressingly crude toilet closet. By the seat-less, age-stained porcelain bowl hung a large grey cloth and below this stood a battered metal bucket and small watering can minus its sprinkler. Both were presently empty. High on the peeling green wall above the bowl was an evidently useless water tank from which dangled the rusted and broken remains of a chain and directly above, on a twisted brown flex, hung a dead-eye light bulb.

As she stood in numbed dismay it took Karen time to realise the bucket and can were the only means, with hot water waiting on the kitchen stove, by which anyone might wash before tipping away used water to help flush the bowl itself. She hesitated only as long as was needed to work out how best to deal with the hot water, using the small pan as a scoop, adding water from the iron pump and to come to terms with what lay in the nightmare closet before her. Choice was not an option but there was, mercifully, a degree of privacy.

Afterwards, for no logical reason she could muster, perhaps to extend her time alone to think, Karen took the cloth and wiped about the top of the bowl.

To a mournful metallic creaking of the iron pump she rinsed her hands under cold water but all of twenty challenging minutes had gone by before she was ready to leave the kitchen. She listened. There was only the sound of dripping water from the pump. Hoping she would remain unobserved, she stepped back into the utility room and to the outer door. There, holding her breath, she teased the thin green curtain open slightly, fearful in case Grimshaw should be waiting outside. Seeing no one, she drew the curtain wider. Through the begrimed glass pane she glimpsed outer buildings backed by woodland with the hills rising beyond against a weeping sky. Not unexpectedly she found this door locked with no key to be seen. About to let the curtain fall back, she hesitated and pressed closer to the glass so as to gaze further out at either side. Partly visible to the right of the door was something she did not expect. 'Oh, Christ,' she gasped, 'it's our car!'

Karen returned through the kitchen, treading cautiously back along the hallway to peer around the door into the main room while attempting not to look directly at the window. There she paused. Mrs Baxendale was no longer seated at the table and from the corner of her eye she became aware that the ogre was no longer visible outside. For heart-beating moments she stared at the outer front door. Could it be unlocked? If it was unlocked then she might be able to leave the house, reach the stable and free Richard. But even if the door was unlocked would she dare to venture outside? No, Grimshaw might be close by so now she hoped the door *was* locked. Karen noted that the shotgun was missing from beside the door where Mrs Baxendale had earlier placed it. She suspected the reason for the shotgun having been taken was because the woman would have it at the stable where she and Grimshaw intended to confront Richard. Mrs Baxendale would meanwhile be expecting her to go upstairs. Was the woman delaying to allow her enough time? To the left of the alcove opposite rested the telephone. Karen glanced again at the window and again at the door, listening, fearing at any moment they could return. She drew breath, stepped quickly across the room, picked up the handset and pressed it to her ear. There was no dialling tone. Only empty silence. Through the window she observed Mrs Baxendale and Grimshaw standing outside the stable where Richard would still be held. If either looked toward the house they would see her so Karen stepped back from the window.

With a renewed sense of dread she returned to the hallway, hesitated, glanced yet again at the front door, then turned to slowly ascend narrow, creaking, uncarpeted stairs. At the top Karen faced a low, ill-lit landing where grey floorboards were part covered by a scattering of patterned, age-worn rugs. The still air carried an odour of musty old furniture but alone in the house, her thoughts were becoming more focussed. She peered about, not knowing what she sought or what she might find but ever hoping for a hint or a clue that could offer a chance of freedom. Along the landing were spaced two dark brown doors with a third facing her at the far end. The first door at her left, the one Mrs Baxendale had mentioned, was part opened. Karen peered inside.

Old, cold and uncared for - that was her first impression. The room, illuminated by a single casement window, was small with faded floral wallpaper, peeling in places beneath a crack-crazed plaster ceiling. There were rugs on otherwise bare floorboards and a fine layer of dust indicated no one had cleaned the room for some time. The single, iron framed bed, taking up almost a quarter of the space, bore lacquered metal head and footboards. Karen likened these latter to prison bars. On the sagging mattress, by a pile of folded sheets and blankets, lay her shoulder bag and holdall, removed from the car as had been Richard's case. To the right of the window stood a plain oak dressing table over which was draped an embroidered white cloth with, positioned above, an oval, hinged mirror. On the cloth were arrayed a number of small ceramic ornaments and a hairbrush. Before the dressing table stood a carved wooden, upright chair. To the other side of the window rested an oak chest of drawers upon which stood a large floral bowl and matching wash jug of Victorian ancestry. Next to these stood a tarnished brass oil lamp with smoke-stained glass funnel but no shade. Perhaps it had been the light from one of these lamps, perhaps this very one, that she and Richard had spotted on that previous, fateful night. There were sounds from outside.

***

The iron bar grated, Mrs Baxendale drew open the left side stable door with Grimshaw standing close behind her. In his right hand he carried the spade, in his left an anonymous bundle.

'Where's Karen!' demanded Richard, moving away from the straw bed to confront the woman as both stepped inside. 'I want to see her so put that bloody gun down and let me out of here!'

'All in good time,' responded the woman as Grimshaw lowered the bundle to the floor. 'Aye, all in good time. Meanwhile,' she continued, gesturing at the bundle, 'I'll 'ave you put on that coat and boots. Tha'll need 'em to keep warm outdoors.'

Richard ignored her words and insisted, 'I want to know where Karen is! I want to see her now, okay - right now!'

Mrs Baxendale moved a step closer and informed him, 'I've done nowt other than keep 'er shut away in't 'ouse for a while. Put on them clothes if you please. The lad and I will wait outside until you're ready then we'll go over to the 'ouse.'

Richard stared back at her in disbelief. 'Like hell I will!' he exclaimed. 'Let me see Karen right now and let us get away from here!'

The woman glared back at him and raising the spade, Grimshaw moved closer as she declared in a voice of shifting gravel, 'You'll put 'em on now. And let me tell you; my lad's already got an eye for that girl of yours, but nowt will 'appen as long as you both be'ave and do as I say. We'll wait outside but not for very long.'

They left Richard alone with the door part open but from where he stood he was able to hear voices, mainly that of the woman. On the stable floor lay a heavy grey coat and a pair of stout but well-worn leather farm worker's boots. Richard looked at them, his mind a maelstrom of anger. He strode to the door and pushed it further open. The two outside turned to him, the woman glaring and levelling her shotgun, the man, with a twisted scowl, raising his spade. 'Put them things on!' the woman demanded. 'Put 'em on or I give it Grimshaw to deal with y'both.'

Richard teetered on the verge of outright refusal, about to once more insist upon his own and Karen's release – but no, it seemed to oppose the woman's demands there and then was not an option. So with the gun still aimed at him, he backed into the stable. There he stood for a time looking at the still open door then, slowly, he removed his shoes, eased on the boots and picked up the coat. The coat would not fit over his jacket so this he slipped off and hung over the end of a wooden partition. He was pulling on the coat when Mrs Baxendale peered around the corner to say, 'Well managed it at last 'ave we - then let's 'ave you out.'

Outside the stable, under a lightly drizzling sky, Richard stood looking at the woman, at the shotgun pointed at his chest and at the mutilated creature that must once have been a man with thoughts and feelings like those of most other men. Mrs Baxendale gestured to the house with the barrel of her gun. Grimshaw moved closer with the spade half raised. Richard knew nothing he could say would help the situation as he turned and walked toward the house, glancing several times at the plainly visible track leading away to the clearing and the road as the pair followed close behind.

***

Karen had closed the bedroom door and stood with bated breath listening to a profound silence - a silence of ages past. Now there were noises from beyond. She moved forward, pushed by a tall, panelled oak wardrobe that faced the end of the bed and stepped across to the window. Easing the age-greyed net curtain aside she had a view through tarnished glass to the stable in which she and Richard had been imprisoned. In the drizzling daylight she observed Mrs Baxendale below with her shotgun raised. There, too, was the ogre carrying his spade in the manner of a warrior ready for combat as they escorted Richard toward the house. Richard looked very different, hair unkempt and dressed now in an incongruous farm worker's coat and boots. She continued to stare out even when the three had disappeared from sight. The misted hills rising beyond offered no comfort. There were no other properties to be seen apart from an abandoned and roofless stone building just visible in the distance. There were no cars, no roads in evidence. She imagined the house standing remote in an endless landscape of despair.

Karen turned to her shoulder bag and holdall. She delved first into the shoulder bag to see if anything had been removed. The contents had obviously been disturbed but the purse containing her money and bankcards was still there. And so was her smart phone. She wondered briefly if Mrs Baxendale had ever seen or even knew what such a device was so her hopes arose as a bright flame. She reached to lift the phone out and switch it on. That flame of hope died for as in the car there was no signal. Even so, she continued to stare at the phone a while longer wishing that, somehow, it would suddenly come alive and allow her to communicate with the outside world. She replaced the phone in her shoulder bag only to discover the contents of her holdall had also been interfered with and one item removed – her make-up bag.

'Why,' muttered Karen, 'what use could the nasty old bitch have with that?' She turned to the dressing table mirror and tilted it up until her sullied image stared back. Her once smart suit was crumpled and smeared with dirt, her hair dishevelled. She picked up the plain wooden hairbrush, turning it about to see if there were any hairs embedded in the bristles. There were none so she sat before the mirror, tilted it down, plied the brush through her hair until satisfied that she appeared moderately presentable. Presentable only to herself, perhaps, to look as she wanted herself to look and not as circumstances dictated. That was reason enough. She arose and stared at the wardrobe. Was she going to change her clothes as she had been ordered and as Richard had obviously done? And if she refused, yes, what if she did, would the consequences be as dire as the woman had threatened? Karen was chilled by the thought of it. She stepped across to open the wardrobe door and peering into its dim interior she encountered a musty, cloying smell that reminded her of an old-style charity shop. Inside were hung old-fashioned gowns and dresses and below these, well-worn slippers and lace-up leather ankle boots. Even her parents did not wear anything quite as dated as these. The clothes appeared to be of average size and she recalled being told they belonged to Mrs Baxendale when she, too, must have been in her twenties or thirties. Karen closed the wardrobe and decided that, although they had forced Richard to do so, she would after all refuse to wear any of these clothes.

***

Once inside the house, Mrs Baxendale pointed out those amenities of which Richard was much in need and where he might wash and shave afterwards in the heat of the kitchen.

Richard dealt as best he was able with the primitive facilities that had confronted him and realised that Karen, too, must have been likewise compromised. On re-entering the kitchen he saw the woman standing outside the door to the hallway. The dark figure of Grimshaw he had observed loitering close outside the rear door of the utility room so assuming this to be unlocked, he did not approach. He thought to obtain a knife from the kitchen but realised the woman was watching him too closely and still retained her shotgun. He turned to the age-crazed mirror, stared at his reflection and noted the tender bruise on his lightly stubbled face where Grimshaw had a second time struck him. 'What the hell have we got ourselves into?' he breathed. 'C'mon, matey, what are you going to do about it? Do something - yes, and do it bloody quick.' And all the time through his mind tumbled the words, 'Karen, where the hell *are* you?'

His thoughts returned to the shotgun. If he could seize it from the woman before the other had opportunity to act then there might be a chance. He could knock her down then quickly work out how to use the gun against Grimshaw. But for now he could only watch and wait. On the shelf above the sink was the dish containing a tablet of soap and by it lay an old safety razor, a wooden-handled, splayed bristle brush and shaving cream in a round ceramic jar. He imagined trying to use these as he stood poised over the sink before the mirror with too little light. He assumed Karen must have been there not so long before as the bar of soap was wet when he picked it up and the towel still damp in spite of heat from the kitchen range. He did not intend to shave. To do so would be a further admission of defeat, an acceptance of the situation they found themselves in. His electric shaver remained in his case, fully charged that previous evening in what had been a world of light and sanity. On passing by, Richard glanced up the staircase and thinking the floor above must be where they were keeping Karen he was tempted to call her name. That temptation wavered under the hostile eye of Mrs Baxendale and the levelled shotgun, yet he hoped that Karen somehow must know he was there.

She insisted Richard must eat at the table in the main room as Karen had been so obliged before him. Mrs Baxendale sat behind, watching quietly from the alcove by the window with the shotgun cradled on her lap. Grimshaw, sheltering beneath the front door porch where he was able to stand fully upright, awaited her summons. Richard, too, remained silent and unwilling even to look at her until Mrs Baxendale said, 'When you've done there, generator int' out'ouse needs fixin'. My Len used to see to that an' always made out it were easy. I never got around to it because it were always 'is job and 'e were right 'andy with anythin' like that.'

'Generator!' Richard exclaimed, twisting about to face her. 'Damn your generator – I do nothing until I see Karen is safe! Is she upstairs?' He assessed the distance between them and again considered his options for action. Could he leap up and get at this gnarled old hag of a woman? Could he wrestle away the gun in time to confront Grimshaw?

Mrs Baxendale seemed to know his thoughts as she swivelled the gun toward him, saying, 'The girl's already eaten and she's waitin' upstairs until she's called. She knows not to come down yet or you both will face problems. Now about the generator -.'

'The generator,' Richard breathed. 'And if I manage to fix this generator of yours, does that mean we get out of here?'

'We've still a good supply of paraffin,' continued Mrs Baxendale, ignoring the question, 'an' there's enough to keep generator goin' all through the winter months an' well beyond if it's used only an hour or two each day whent' weather's cold.' Richard was about to repeat his question when she added, 'There's lots of jobs for both of you - aye, lots that needs doin'. There's that fence over by the quarry to be fixed back in place before any sheep wanders over the edge. Aye, it all 'as to be done now you two are 'ere.'

Richard glanced again at the shotgun before turning slowly back to the table where he gripped the knife and thought hard about what he might do.

***

Karen stepped to the bedroom door, opened it cautiously and peered along the deserted landing. There were noises downstairs – a creaking sound she knew was from the iron pump, doors closing then voices - one of them a man's; one she recognised. She was reassured in the certainty of it being Richard, but in spite of an all but irrepressible urge to do so she feared the consequences if she called out to him or if she dashed down the stairs. The murderous Grimshaw would surely be there. She stood listening. A door slammed. Then silence.

A minute had passed before she crept slowly along to the next room, wishing she had removed her soiled high heels as they tapped on bare wood between the rugs. She still hoped there might be something worthwhile, some clue, some item that might suggest a means of escape. The second door opened with a mouse squeak to reveal a bedroom cleaner, well-kept and slightly larger than that allocated to her; evidently the one used by Mrs Baxendale though it possessed little more in the way of furnishing and decoration than the dismal room she had minutes ago left. There on the dressing table was another oil lamp and close about it were carefully arranged a crucifix, a small prayer book and a number of gilded-framed black and white photographs, some blemished, others faded. Karen stepped closer to peer at the photographs. Here, both standing before a church entrance, was a bright-eyed and smiling young woman in traditional wedding dress together with her smartly suited, dark-haired groom. Here were full-length views and close-up portraits of a man and a woman in later stages of life and Karen recognised a pensive Mrs Baxendale of middle years. There were no children. Set aside from the rest was a photograph of the farm as it must have appeared in earlier days; in their youth, perhaps. The nature of these things and the manner in which they were arranged had Karen wondering if the dressing table was an altar of memories, the very room itself a shrine to the woman's past life. She turned quietly away and stepped back onto the landing.

The door facing her at the end of the landing proved to be the bathroom. Tarnished brass taps and fittings contrasted with discoloured white tiles, some of them cracked, and an ancient enamel bath that contained dust and paint flakes fallen like white butterflies from the ceiling. It was also the final resting place for a large black spider. Above the bath was suspended a wooden rack intended for drying clothes, with the cord to raise and lower it wound around a metal cleat further down on the wall. More noises arose from downstairs and were followed by the sound of another door slamming. This, she suspected, was the main door at the front of the house.

Karen returned quickly along the landing to the first room and to the window where she hoped she might see Richard again but there was no one in sight. She decided to do nothing until the woman returned. She determined she would try again to reason with her in the hope that matters had not gone beyond reason. She glanced at her watch to see the time was eight twenty-five so she swung the upright chair around to face the door and sat to wait and listen. Little more than five minutes had passed before the stairs began to creak. Quietly at first. Closer. Then louder. The door swung open and there stood Mrs Baxendale. The woman eyed her angrily and demanded, 'Why've you not changed, girl? I told you to change and you have not!'

'Stop it!' cried Karen, rising abruptly to her feet. 'Stop this stupid game! How long d'you think it can go on? You've held us against our will and you've even stolen from me! Let's end this now and let both of us leave!'

'Stolen!' exclaimed the woman. 'All I've taken from thee are the temptations of vanity. There's no place for vanity in this 'ouse. Disobey me girl,' she hissed, 'and as I've made clear to you already I'll 'ave Grimshaw sort things out, startin' with that man of yours. What 'as to be done 'as to be done so *you* must get on an' do as *you're* told!'

'I want to see Richard – don't you understand! I know he was downstairs just now.' The woman continued to stare at her so Karen lowered her voice, saying, 'All right, if - if I do as you ask with those old clothes will you let me go to him?'

Mrs Baxendale moved closer, a gleam of fierce determination in her grotesquely magnified eyes. 'Aye, do as you're told and you'll see 'im in good time. But if there's any funny business from 'im or from you, as God is my witness, my Grimshaw will take that fancy man of yours apart. It won't bother 'im in the least because 'e knows not right from wrong any more so can never bear the burden of guilt. Understand this, girl - we 'ave nothin' to lose. No, nothin' at all! We'll go right on as before you came even though the work gets ever 'arder; even though it brings me closer to my maker. Aye, there's only so much of a burden I can carry as 'im above knows.'

Karen felt very afraid as she responded, 'You mean you'll have that beast of a man murder Richard. That's what you're saying isn't it - Richard and then me!'

The woman backed toward the door but continued to stare at her. Fearing even more for Richard as she did for herself, Karen turned, trembling, to the wardrobe where she opened the door and again looked inside. This seemed to placate Mrs Baxendale who said, 'If you want to be with 'im, girl, then you'll 'ave to share the stable at night. It's not so pleasant int' stable but I'll not 'ave you livin' in sin together in this 'ouse.' She took hold of the door handle, adding, 'This is the last time I'll ask you to get changed, girl. There won't be another, no there will not.' She stepped back onto the landing then added, 'Oh, and by the way, I 'eard you walkin' about a few minutes ago, nosin' into other rooms. You'll not keep nothin' from me, girl – nothin' at all.'

Mrs Baxendale left, slamming the door hard to emphasise her demands and this time a key rattled in the lock. The stairs creaked and Karen breathed, 'I've got to do as she says or they'll kill us both – I know they will. Richard – Richard - Richard – what the bloody hell are we going to do?'

Karen moved to the locked door, wondering if she might hear Richard's voice again. Perhaps he had never left and was still down there. Hearing nothing other than vague sounds she returned to the wardrobe and drew from its sombre depths a thick cotton ankle-length floral dress with wide white collar and white belt. She slipped off and laid her begrimed suit carefully across the bed, unclipped her silver locket then removed her white blouse. The dress she found strange; its style, its loose fit and the way it swayed heavily about her legs just above the ankles. Next the shoes; not shoes for fashion, not for walking the town or even the village street, but for a working day about the farm. As for her high heels, they represented everything, style, glamour and the good life, everything impossibly alien to this harsh and despairing world. Lastly, she picked up her locket, turned to face the mirror, raised and fastened the small, awkwardly delicate clasp at the back of her neck. She stepped over to the window and waited. It seemed too much time, agonising time, had passed before stairs again began to creak.

**

The geese cackled loudly as Richard, protected by the heavy coat Mrs Baxendale had unearthed for his use, followed her from the stable through a light but chilling drizzle with Grimshaw close behind. With each step Richard was sorely tempted to halt and challenge her but knew he would achieve nothing. He was quite sure the woman would not hesitate to use the shotgun or have Grimshaw set about him with the ever-threatening spade. He nevertheless hesitated as passing by the house they reached the rear of the building where to one side of the back door stood the hired car. He stared and the sight of it stirred a glimmer of hope: was the vehicle equipped with a tracking device? Would the hire company have the police searching for it? That ephemeral light extinguished as he recalled the hire terms. The car was on a seven-day lease. For the coming week his whereabouts and that of Karen would be of no consequence whatsoever to the outside world.

'I've not time to waste,' came her flinty voice and Richard's spine tingled for he sensed the barrels of her gun raised toward him. They continued close by the car to the door of a small stone building attached to the rear of the house. Mrs Baxendale stepped by to unlatch and open the door then gestured for Richard to enter. In the confined space, illuminated by a large window opposite, stood the main feature of the room, the generator, and close by it some dozen or more large plastic containers filled with what Richard assumed must be paraffin. An abundance of cobwebs told him nothing much had been attended to in there for some time. As he looked about, Mrs Baxendale said, 'There you are, there's the toolbox my Len used so 'appen I'll let you get on with it. There's plenty of light int' place so I'll close the door.' Before the door closed completely she peered through the gap to inform him, 'The lad will wait outside and when you're done 'e'll see you back to the 'ouse. Take tha time.'

The door closed, he could hear her speaking to Grimshaw but was unable to make out what was said. And if hope of escape was not revived at least he had time alone in daylight to think. And there was the old wooden toolbox - it might contain something he could use as a weapon. He stooped to release the catch and lift the lid, muttering, 'If I can see to that big bastard outside while she's not looking maybe I can get back to the house and deal with her as well.'

But the modest sized toolbox proved no more than a source of disappointment. He lifted out a hammer; the sole implement he considered might be of use. It was a light hammer and one blow against a man like Grimshaw, no matter how hard, might not be enough. He stepped to the smaller window next to the door and looked out to see the man standing not two metres away. Grimshaw spotted him and moved closer. His face transformed into a bizarrely misshapen grin as he raised and shook the spade in both hands. Richard stepped back from the window, replaced the hammer, gazed down at the toolbox, closed the lid and breathed, 'It'll take more than anything in there to lay the bugger out.'

He turned to look at the generator and remained occupied in thought. This was his first encounter with a generator. He walked around it, peered closer then stepped back. Richard regarded it as a wounded mechanical beast; one he had not the means of reviving. Reaching down he touched and handled parts of the machine until his fingers were soiled with grease and dirt. A cloth hung from a nearby hook and with this he wiped the excess from his hands. 'Hope the bloody woman'll be convinced,' he murmured. But for now he must wait. He must have her think he was attempting to do as she demanded.

Grimshaw was standing further away when Richard at last emerged from the outhouse. The sky had brightened, the wind had freshened and carried with it the mournful sound he and Karen already knew. He stood three paces from Grimshaw, wondering what next to do, then decided to make his way back to the house. Grimshaw followed dutifully then Mrs Baxendale, seeing them approach, appeared at the rear door. Evidently Richard was not to be allowed into the house.

'Is it fixed then?' she asked as he stopped before her.

'I've checked the thing over,' he replied, holding out his hands to emphasise the grime. 'It's seized up completely. It needs stripping down by a qualified engineer.'

'Oh it does, does it!' she exclaimed. 'Well my Len never needed a ruddy engineer!'

'Well maybe that's why it needs one now!' he responded, much tempted to seize her by the throat.

Mrs Baxendale glanced at his hands, saying, 'Then we'll 'ave to try again later, won't we. I've plenty of candles left but they 'ave to be conserved because when they're gone there'll be no light after sunset other than two or three oil lamps – aye, just like it were in the old days. Anyway, there's other things to be done before you wash those gentlemanly 'ands of yours. You can do what my Grimshaw's been doin' but without my supervision. The rain's cleared up so you can get along and dig out a few potatoes or you and the girl will get nowt for dinner. I'm sure you'll manage that. There's a sack and spade int' green'ouse. Garden needs a bit of diggin' over afterwards but don't get no fancy ideas with the spade and don't forget where that girl of yours is. She'll be 'elpin' with other things in 'ere now she's dressed for work.'

'What d'you mean by that?' Richard demanded. 'What sort of work?'

'Work int' kitchen and jobs around this 'ouse, that's what I mean. I've enough to do with 'ens,

137

geese and two cows, an' those few sheep I 'ave left seldom get looked at.'

'I want to talk to Karen now,' he insisted. 'A few minutes – what harm can that do?'

Ignoring his request she looked past him at Grimshaw, saying, 'Watch over 'im int' garden won't you, lad. Make sure all the tools are put back where they belong an' don't you stand for any funny business.'

'N-no, Ma,' Grimshaw growled softly, grasping the spade as his gaze fixed hard upon Richard, 'no funny b-business or I knock 'im down 'ard.'

***

Karen was seated by the table in the front room of the house when Mrs Baxendale returned to stand facing her. 'Your fancy man's about 'is work with my Grimshaw,' she announced, 'so now's the time for me to show you 'ow to clean out and fire up the woodstove and 'ow food is best prepared on it, then I can get on with the many other things that I 'ave to do. We've enough matches, my Len saw to that, but they're not to be wasted. You'll later learn to 'elp with milkin' cows but killin' geese and 'ens I'll deal with. Can't get blood on those pretty 'ands of yours can we. At least not yet.'

Listening to those words a sudden consuming anger seized Karen. Hands gripping the edge of the table she part rose and cried, 'That's enough! This crazy theatre of yours has to stop! We're real people, not bloody slaves! We have to go from here! We have to take our things and leave now!' Just listen to me – we have to take our own clothes, we have to get into our car and go!'

Her expression gargoyle-grim, Mrs Baxendale strode forward, raised her right arm, struck Karen hard across the face and snarled, 'Tha'll not swear within these walls!' Karen reeled back with a cry, a hand clasped to her cheek as she stumbled against her chair causing it to overturn and clatter to the floor. She glared at the woman with a burning anger beyond anything she had known then reached to seize the bread knife. Mrs Baxendale stepped back as Karen, knife raised, moved around the table. 'This is where it ends!' she declared. 'Call that beast of a man away from Richard! Keep him away from both of us! I know our car's outside so give me the keys! Give them to me now!'

Mrs Baxendale, with measured calmness, replied in an abrasive whisper, 'How dare you deny the Lord's will. Try to use that knife on me, girl, and Grimshaw will break your fancy man's neck wi'out a second thought. Then as surely as I stand 'ere 'e'll break thy neck as well - unless 'e does what 'e pleases with you first; after all when it comes t'basics 'e's still a man. D'you understand what I'm sayin', girl - do you?'

Karen remained facing her with the knife raised for heart-pounding seconds, then at last she breathed, 'Yes, I understand you only too well.' The fire in the grate cracked as wood settled and, slowly, she lowered the knife. Mrs Baxendale continued to stare at her then announced calmly, 'I'll explain about the stove, then like I said, I 'ave to go and see to other things. I'll come back later then we'll get down to further business.'

139

Karen, perplexed and numbed, was ushered to the kitchen and said nothing more as Mrs Baxendale explained how the iron stove was to be cleaned and prepared. The woman left her but Karen moved to watch from the end of the hallway as Mrs Baxendale picked up the shotgun and pulled open the front door. As the door closed, Karen pressed hands tightly to her smarting face. Tears seeped through her fingers as she returned to the kitchen, there to ask quietly, 'Oh, god, Richard, where are you - what are we going to do?'

As twilight encroached upon the valley Karen was confined to the locked upstairs room, knowing that Richard was down below eating the meal she had been obliged to prepare; one of boiled potatoes, green vegetables and thin slices of chicken washed down by cold water. The food had drawn no comment of approval or otherwise from Mrs Baxendale. Karen stood by the bedroom door listening to sporadic voices downstairs, mainly that of Mrs Baxendale. She heard the front door close, then watched from the window as Richard was escorted to the stable. She was sorely tempted to bang with her fists on the glass, to smash it and to scream her anger at those below. But at what cost?

Downstairs, a short time later, Karen had to sit and eat facing Mrs Baxendale with Grimshaw seated only an arm's length away at the end of the table to her right, noisily chewing food, some of which fell from his twisted mouth. Much of the time Grimshaw's eyes were fixed upon Karen while throughout the meal, gripped by fear, she kept her gaze resolutely away from him and on her plate.

She found the situation all but impossible to bear, felt herself close to breaking point, all the while desperate to be out of the house and with Richard. The meal was mercifully at an end. Karen cleared away the dishes in silence, relieved by the fact that Mrs Baxendale passed across to her those used by Grimshaw. She knew perfectly well why the ogre had been allowed to sit there, realised fully that his presence was intended to discourage further defiance. Inside the kitchen, out of Grimshaw's sight, she ladled hot water from the big copper pan into the sink. There, cloth in hand, trembling and fearful, she washed the dishes before attending to her personal needs in the odious closet adjoining the utility room.

When returning Karen to the stable with Grimshaw close behind, Mrs Baxendale said, 'I'll 'ave you and the lad eat separate in future as long as you be'ave.'

'Will you now,' muttered Karen. 'Will you really.'

**

They sat hand in hand in diminishing light. They listened to the echoing scrape of the iron bar as it sealed shut the doors of their stone prison. Neither spoke for some time then Karen said, 'Richard, it's taken them a day, only a day, and look what they've done to us. And have you seen the car? She'll have hidden the keys well out of sight so somehow – somehow, we have to get back to the road. Richard, how are we going to get away from this awful place?'

'Karen, love, right now I really don't know and yes, I have seen the car. That big grinning bastard was never more than a few feet away from me with that spade of his. If I'd tried anything I'm damned sure he'd have whacked me with it because that's what she's programmed him to do. You've been in that house most of the day haven't you; what's been happening?'

'I - I grabbed a knife earlier. I was going to kill her. I know I could have done it and I didn't care. Then - then she said that dreadful man would murder both of us just as you said he would. I had to do as she told me for both our sakes.' Karen sighed then continued, 'I had to use that disgusting toilet of hers then clean around it. There was no sign of any disinfectant and if she ever stored up any toilet paper, well it's all gone now. There was just a can with a spout. I had to ladle hot water out of the pan to fill the thing so I could wash myself then use what was left and a part-filled bucket of water from the pump to flush the bowl. At least there was a bar of soap.'

'No need to go through it all,' muttered Richard, 'I've been in there as well.'

'Yes, I - yes, of course you have,' she sighed.

'No choice was there. But surely that big bugger can't go in there.'

'And that filthy woodstove; I had to clean the ashes out before I managed to get the thing going. She took the ashes to the greenhouse then came back and stood over me and told me I hadn't done the stove properly and I'd better get it right next time and - and if I didn't do as she said, yet again,

142

she wouldn't be responsible for what might happen to either of us. She said she had the geese, the chickens and the rest of the farm to look after and I had to clean out the house because she'd never had enough time to do it. After that she went outside again and locked the outer doors. I don't think anyone's been over some of that house in ages, not her, not anyone. All she does is farm work.'

'Well,' said Richard, 'she had me trying to get her bloody generator started. I tell you I wouldn't know one end of a generator from the other so I got my hands messed up to make it look as if I really had made the effort. Then after she'd taken out her cows she had me shovel out the cowshed then dig out the damned potatoes – both filthy bloody jobs with her gorilla standing guard while she buggered off somewhere else. I saw her disappear into one of the outbuildings for a time but I don't know what goes on in there. She'd made it abundantly clear at the start how they'd take it out on you if I didn't get on with what she wanted.'

There was further silence. Both looked up at a darkening sky through the two small windows above then Karen said, 'The food they brought in to you - I had to prepare it from a chicken she'd killed and plucked earlier and she told me I'd soon have to learn how to do that as well. I had to eat with them both. Yes, and *he* was staring at me all the time with food dropping out of his mouth when he tried to talk. She had him there on purpose to scare me – I know she did. Richard it - it was horrible, really horrible. I wanted to scream and she knew it because she said when they were bringing me back here she'd let me eat without him being there if I did as she wanted. This is all madness - utter, utter madness!'

'Karen, love, we have to play this cool. We have to go along with her until we see a chance of – of doing something.'

'Yes, I – I'll try. But soon, Richard, it has to be soon.'

'Is that ape-man her son, or what?' Richard asked.

'No, she told me about that. She wanted to explain everything so I understood what had happened, why they are here and why she can't ever allow us to leave.'

'Can't ever allow us to -!' Richard exclaimed.

'She's been trying to run the farm with the ogre's help but there's only so much he can do without her being there. He has the mind of a child.'

'Not like any child I ever met,' responded Richard. 'More like something Frankenstein put together in dim light. What else did she tell you, Karen? There must be a hell of a lot more to this than I've been able to figure out.'

'Richard, she thinks we've been sent by God to help keep her farm going. She actually believes we're a gift from heaven.'

'Well I'm not a gift from anywhere and neither are you. The woman is totally mad!'

'Mad, Richard? Yes, mad or utterly deluded.'

'Deluded – mad, what's the difference! From what you've said she regards us as a permanent asset, as if all this had been worked out in advance –

as if she'd been expecting us. Karen, I really need to know everything you learned.'

In the now pervading darkness Karen could no longer see his face so she squeezed his hand tighter. 'Right now, Richard, I can hardly think straight. I don't want to say any more about it until my mind is clear – not until tomorrow.'

'Don't want -!' he exclaimed. 'But you have to!'

Richard, no! I feel so very tired and confused. I just need to sleep. I want to hide away and forget. I want to wake up and find none of this is true.'

'All right, Karen, I won't insist but pretty soon I have to know as much as you. What's more I feel totally ashamed of myself for letting this happen and being so bloody incapable of sorting it out. Really I do.'

There was no response. Richard listened for a while to Karen's breathing and knew she had fallen asleep.

Chapter 5

Karen awoke to the sound of rain tap-dancing on the slate roof above. She was cold and pulled the blanket more closely about herself. Richard still slept, breathing lightly. She gazed into the obscurity of the stable and at the small windows above where early morning light offered no comfort. She assessed their situation. Who could ever guess where she and Richard were? They had told no one of their plans. They had booked nothing ahead. There were tales of people who disappeared never to be seen again; people who once walked, talked and laughed but then were only a statistic. Nothing.

She waited a while before whispering close to his ear, 'Richard, wake up.'

He stirred, groaned, opened his eyes, drew breath, looked at her and about the stable then sighed, 'What a mess I've got us into, Karen – what a bloody awful mess.'

'Don't blame yourself, Richard, this could have happened to anyone.'

'Happen to -! Well it didn't happen to anyone did it, Karen, it happened to us; a one chance in millions and it happened to us.' He sat up, peered at his watch then said, 'It's getting on for seven o'clock. Have you heard anything outside?'

'No, nothing, just the rain but it sounds now like that's easing off. I woke up earlier for a few minutes; it was still dark so I had no idea what time it was. I could hear that noise, like some kind of mournful chorus drifting out of the night. That's what the damned woman hears, you know. It's what she thinks is the voice of God telling her what to do. She must know we can hear it as well.'

'Voice of God,' he sighed. 'People like that are the worst. They think something up there is on their side even when their worst enemy thinks exactly the same. They've lost all sense of reason.'

'I was convinced yesterday she really would use her gun on us.' Karen said. 'But what if we just refused to do anything? What if we refused to move or – or what if we just walked away – do you think she still might -?'

'Yes I do,' he cut in, 'or just as likely she'd have him do her dirty work. I'd only chance getting away from here if I was on my own then I'd make a run for it.' Richard struggled to his feet, pulled on his clothes, his socks and boots then dragged about himself the old coat that he, like Karen, had been given. 'You've got to talk to me, haven't you,' he said, 'about yesterday - about what she told you.'

'Yes, before they come and separate us, I'll tell you as much as I can for now.'

Karen offered a hurried outline of what Mrs Baxendale had told her and Richard said, 'So they tried to murder the poor bloody security man but turned him into Grimshaw instead. Look, I'm going to try those doors before they get here. They'll probably be locked but still I have to try. I *have* to do something!' But he had taken only few steps away from their makeshift beds when footsteps were heard outside and the rasping scrape of the iron bar echoed through the stable. Richard stopped then Karen was by his side, grasping his arm. As on

147

that previous morning, when the doors part opened, they were confronted by two figures. Mrs Baxendale held the shotgun levelled at Richard with the grotesquely leering Grimshaw standing close at her right.

'Now I've seen to milkin't' cows and much else,' the woman announced, 'I'll deal with you two. Come on out, girl,' she ordered, gesturing to Karen. 'You'd better be first.'

Karen hesitated, drew the coat more closely about herself, glanced aside at Richard then stepped into grey morning light beneath a still weeping sky. The mutilated man, an insane grin crumpling his face, stared at her and breathed, 'P-pretty lady.'

'Grimshaw,' ordered Mrs Baxendale, 'close and bar that door, there's a good lad.'

Parody of an obedient child, Grimshaw lumbered up to the doors. Karen watched Richard's image vanish as the door clattered shut and the bar was slid back into position. 'Good lad,' said Mrs Baxendale as Grimshaw returned, stammering the words, 'I c-closed it good. Is th-that all right, Ma?'

'Yes, lad, that's very good,' she replied, then turned to Karen who stood shivering in spite of the heavy coat. 'Now you go an' do your necessaries int' back then prepare yourself and your man a bite to eat. Finish yours then go to the upstairs room and wait until I call for you. I already 'ave the stove goin' but as of today that'll be your job each mornin'.'

'What's happening to Richard?' Karen demanded.

'Your fancy man goes in't back after you. He'll do 'is necessaries then take 'is breakfast while you wait int' upstairs room, then there's work for 'im to do outside. He can get back t'that generator and try again to get it goin'. Yes, 'e'll 'ave to try a bit 'arder. Now get along, girl, if y'don't mind.'

Karen hurried to the house with Grimshaw several steps behind and all the time she sensed his baleful gaze burning into her. In the kitchen, with the door closed, she felt a degree of relief on finding the woodstove had been burning long enough to ensure the large copper pan of water standing on it was adequately heated. There was a frayed green curtain and this she pulled across to cover the kitchen window. And there was still the bar of soap by the kitchen sink. Karen peered about to see if there was some object, anything that might hold a clue to their salvation, all the time knowing Mrs Baxendale waited outside. Stacked on one of the shelves in the utility room, above the long dead refrigerator and equally useless washing machine, she noted what she had failed to see the previous day, some twenty or more tablets of soap. These small items she assumed must have been obtained in excess among other essentials by Mrs Baxendale's husband before his death. But once again she would be obliged to make the best of those primitive and degrading facilities she so dreaded.

On preparing herself as best she was able, Karen saw hanging just inside the locked outer door the plucked carcase of a chicken she guessed had been killed that morning, but for the time being she

149

would find only milk, bread and cheese to satisfy her hunger. To her relief she was left alone at the table, all the time looking about the room, all the time pondering upon the situation and wondering where Richard might presently be.

Mrs Baxendale returned to the house via the front door as Karen finished eating and said, 'Now then, girl, get upstairs and get thaself into fresh clothes.'

Karen stared at her but did not move from the table until the woman appeared once more ready to deliver threats. Seething within, she left the room, ascended the stairs and re-entered to where her holdall still lay on the unused bed. Footsteps on the stairs were followed moments later by the door closing behind her and the sound of a key scraping in the lock. The footsteps retreated. Karen stood to gaze across to the widow and a cloying silence fell upon her. She remained as she was until hearing noises from below. She stepped to the wardrobe, opened the door and there she gazed into its melancholy depths. The gaping darkness before which she stood might have been an open coffin. Karen closed her eyes and in those pensive minutes time and space wavered. Gone was the darkness, gone the musty, faded clothes of a bygone age and there instead a vision of the world from which she had little more than a week ago departed. There was the villa in Languedoc, there the sunlit Mediterranean hills and vineyards and there the covert pleasures of which she dared not speak. Were those she had left behind thinking of her? Did they wonder if or when she would return? She raised hands to her cheeks and whispered, 'Oh god, what has happened to me; I once knew a house of angels and now I find myself in a house of hell.' She reached out, fancying that if she were to step forward she might pass through a hidden portal and into to a glorious world of sunlit gardens, blue sea and summer breezes.

The vision wavered. A door slammed and there were further sounds from below. Karen opened her eyes and was again feeling cold. She drew out more clothes: old but warmer clothes including that icon of a twilight generation, a cardigan. She returned to her holdall. In there nestled an assortment of personal items including spare lingerie, a pack of moist tissues and a tube of hand cream. None of these modest items had Mrs Baxendale considered worthy of confiscation. Karen changed her clothes and there were voices downstairs. There was Richard's voice. It could only be Richard. She stepped to the door, forgetting it had been locked, intending to wrench it open, to call his name and to hurry down the stairs regardless of the consequences. But the door still was locked.

A fraught half hour of uncertainty passed before she heard the door unlock and there stood Mrs Baxendale, light from the window opposite glinting from her glasses. 'I 'ope we 'ave more luck with the generator this time around,' she declared. 'Your fancy man is back in there now.'

'Generators are *not* a part of his business!' snapped Karen.

'No, girl,' countered the woman, 'neither were it part of my Len's, God rest 'is soul, but he

151

managed it all the same. You can set about doin' up 'ere tomorrow. This mornin' there's washin' to deal with and lunch to be got, then later this afternoon there's a chicken to be boned and prepared for the evenin' meal – I'm sure you'll be able to manage that 'omely little task or 'ave you never cooked anythin' in y'life before. No, I dare say you'll be a stranger to 'onest toil. My Len used to say the air the up 'ere inspired 'ard work and cleansed the soul but I don't suppose it'll do owt for you two?'

'It's cold and miserable exactly like you!' Karen exclaimed, stepping back in anticipation of an angry response.

'Aye, girl, cold it may be on occasion,' was the woman's bland comment, 'but 'olesome an' clean as the Almighty intended. Today I've work a'plenty to do outdoors so -.'

She turned to leave and Karen, knowing she was to follow, eyed her with a scorn deeper than mere words could express.

***

Assailed by the heat of the kitchen range, Karen had with difficulty produced four lunchtime meals. Her watch told her it was almost one-fifteen as now she sat alone at the table with boiled potatoes, boiled eggs and bread set before her. One plate had been taken by Mrs Baxendale and Grimshaw to the stable where Richard was again imprisoned, the second and third to one of the outbuildings where Karen had earlier concluded Grimshaw himself had to be housed. It was there, she reasoned, the ogre must sleep and it was there Mrs Baxendale must care for him, for care in a number of ways he must need. Karen suspected which building he occupied since she had observed one of the larger outhouses to have a chimney rising above the roof, so there had to be a fireplace. Was it, she wondered, originally the residence for a farm worker and his family? Was there a source of water in there – another pump, perhaps? Did she wash and clean for Grimshaw, did she assist this profoundly damaged brute of a man with those essentials of life most people took for granted they would cope with? The thought of what Mrs Baxendale might have to do for him touched her with a profound revulsion.

Karen tried hard to think upon other matters. She recalled the events of earlier that morning when she had appeared downstairs to assist Mrs Baxendale in the kitchen. One of the tasks imposed upon her had been to boil water to aid in washing an assortment of clothes. These were placed into a galvanised bin, repeatedly charged with hot and cold water then churned about with a broom pole. They were individually rinsed in the cold sink before being passed through the rusting, crank-turned mangle then carried upstairs to be draped over the wooden rack in the otherwise useless bathroom. It was gruelling, tiresome work and Mrs Baxendale allowed too little soap because her store of this precious item could never be replenished. Karen wondered what would happen when there was no soap left.

The bin of used water, far too heavy for her or even Richard to handle, had been manoeuvred, rolled on its edge outside and emptied by Grimshaw, then he and Mrs Baxendale had left her alone to prepare lunch. His gaze once more beset Karen's thoughts, a gaze that told of subconscious urges fermenting deep within the man's crippled mind, a leering, elemental gaze that instilled within her a fear unlike any she had known since the nightmares of childhood.

At one-point Mrs Baxendale hurried back into the kitchen to confront Karen in spiteful anger.

'That ruddy man of yours still 'asn't fixed the generator! He knows nowt about real work does 'e! No, nowt at all – d'you 'ear me, girl! But 'e'll find out in due course, aye, because 'e 'as to. Mark my words! Just you mark my words!'

Karen wanted to scream at her, wanted to wrench open the kitchen drawer where the knives were kept, wanted to take up one of them and strike deeply into her again and again and again until the woman lay torn, bleeding and dead at her feet! But she caught her breath, held back and stood with arms at her side, fists clenched and eyes closed until Mrs Baxendale had left her once more alone. Then a thought! Was there any pepper here? She glanced about, opening and closing drawers and cupboard doors, muttering, 'I should have thought of that, shouldn't I – yes, I should have thought of it before now.' If there was pepper she could easily smuggle some out to Richard. He could use it to blind the ogre, to throw it into his face and render him helpless when they were out of Mrs Baxendale's sight – she could use it on Mrs Baxendale herself so then she and Richard could flee. Karen searched, but there was no pepper.

***

It was after lunch when they came to the stable. Richard, seated on the straw bed and leaning against the wall scrambled to his feet as the bar slid aside and one of the doors was dragged open. Mrs Baxendale stood against the light with her shotgun. She looked at him then backed out of sight. It was obvious she expected Richard to exit the stable and so he stepped outside into a chill wind to be confronted by her and by Grimshaw.

'That ruddy generator still isn't fixed!' the woman exclaimed. 'Why's it not?'

'I told you, didn't I,' responded Richard, 'nobody can repair it without spare parts and the right tools. The thing is seized up - okay! Seized up completely - get it!'

'So *you* say,' she declared, 'but you need to think 'ard about it. Meanwhile you can go over to the quarry an' look at the fencin' where some of the posts are down an' see what 'as to be done. My Len would 'ave fixed them up again in case any of the sheep wandered too close but I'm sure you can deal with it. Aye, it's work any man can manage I'd say, so don't come back 'ere an' tell me it needs a ruddy engineer because I'll 'ave none of it - do you understand? Grimshaw will be with you and that girl of yours will be busy int' 'ouse.' She turned to Grimshaw, saying, 'Now, lad, you've to take this man to the quarry, remember? You've to watch 'im for as long as it takes but don't let 'im wander too far away. When 'e's ready, make sure 'e comes back 'ere with you. Is that all right, lad – is it?'

'Th-that's all right, Ma, I'll do that. I'll b-bring 'im back 'ere for you.' He looked at Richard and shook the spade. A drooling grin creased his face as he added, 'If 'e don't do 'as you said th-then I'll knock 'im d-down an' mm-make 'im stay still.'

From the silence that followed arose a mournful wailing. Mrs Baxendale looked reverently up to the sky then switched her attention back to Grimshaw, saying, 'Off you both go then; there's enough time to see what needs doin' over there. Aye, there's enough time now't weather's dry.'

Mrs Baxendale hurried back toward the house, clutching her shotgun. Grimshaw stared threateningly at Richard, gestured with a sweep of his spade toward rising ground beyond the farm buildings then lumbered on, hesitating, looking over his shoulder to see that Richard followed. Richard, pulling the coat about himself, was indeed following but not too close behind. They proceeded for some minutes over grassy, gently rising land where jagged little intrusions of limestone betrayed the thinness of the soil. Richard noted the small number of sheep grazing placidly. His knowledge of sheep he would have admitted was minimal at best but these did not appear the well-kept colour-coded specimens he had casually noted when passing through countryside elsewhere. Then there was the sound that had distracted Mrs Baxendale - louder now than it had been only minutes before. Further along on higher, more exposed ground where the wind was stronger, it filled the air as a soaring elemental requiem. It was for Richard a moment of revelation when he observed the source: a cluster of grass-edged, pale rocks, a natural limestone formation over a metre high. Two of the larger stones were almost vertical, facing one another and curving gently inward to a rough approximation of hands held in prayer. The wind, he realised, was passing through to resonate within the natural cavity formed between these rocks. Here was the source of Mrs Baxendale's celestial voices, allegedly the reason why he and Karen had been rendered victims to her irrational zeal. Richard paused to look closer at the formation, thinking the woman must have always known the source of the sounds but chose to interpret them as messages from a deity she so reverently believed was calling to her.

Grimshaw turned, aware of Richard having stopped. He raised the spade, pointed it at Richard and called, 'Y-you 'ave to do as Ma says!'

The fence lay some way ahead, running directly across the skyline. The gap was obvious even from a distance – a wide gap that looked, as they approached closer, as if some large object had swept part of the fence away. On reaching the rise across which the fence ran, the level ground ended abruptly and the immense void of the quarry opened alarmingly wide in front of him. Richard looked for clues as to what might have damaged the fence but the ground before the area consisted in part of exposed limestone and could tell him nothing. As most of the fence appeared intact, or at worst some of the posts adjacent to the damaged part were tilted and needed straightening, he focussed his attention upon the section where it appeared two posts had once stood. One of the posts lay on its side, shattered, but the other was nowhere to be seen.

Here was an opportunity to think, to consider the situation, so Richard, seeing that Grimshaw presently watched him from several paces away while seated on a near horizontal stone slab, decided to wander up and down along the edge of the quarry as though occupied in assessing what needed to be done. He glanced aside at Grimshaw and his thoughts became whispered words. 'If I can get him close to the edge then maybe, just maybe I could -.' But he had, of course, never attempted to murder anyone and the dire consequences of failure to himself and to Karen loomed immediately real. He continued to stroll casually back and forth, pausing, stooping now and again as if to examine the damaged area closer.

Grimshaw so far had appeared unconcerned about the passing time but Richard, noting how much of the afternoon had gone by, half expected to see Mrs Baxendale appear with her shotgun at the ready and demanding to know why he had not returned with a verbal assessment. He strode up to the gap is if to appraise the situation in greater detail, hesitated, then stepped a short way through. Most of the quarry was now visible, its far walls terraced by excavations from top to bottom, but Richard, not enamoured of unguarded heights, was reluctant to venture nearer to the edge. One thing far below, however, attracted his attention: close to a scattering of discarded equipment stood a wooden shed. The shed was probably empty but anything under present circumstances, anything, no matter how insignificant, seemed worth investigation.

'There's got to be a way down there,' he breathed, treading as close as he dared to the edge and much concerned about the steady breeze that threatened to affect his balance. From where he stood, Richard was able to peer along the whole length of the fence. He noted how, some way further on, it turned abruptly right to continue a short way until terminating at a rock face. This, he concluded, marked the division between farmland and one-time quarry jurisdiction. Beyond this shorter run of fence the ground fell away to reveal, at the far end of the quarry, an earthen ramp that must have served as access for heavy vehicles entering and leaving. Moving back from the edge he observed Grimshaw had risen to his feet and was watching him intently. It was time to return and face the intimidating gaze of Mrs Baxendale.

***

Karen had been obliged to undertake the time-consuming task of heating more water over the woodstove, then possessed only of a cotton cloth and bar of soap, cleaning plates, dishes and cutlery. And although the kitchen was uncomfortably warm at times it was at least preferable to the changeable weather outside. The tube of hand cream and packet of moist tissues she carried on her person. The hand cream in particular, resting for now by the sink, was among those few items she would employ with utmost care.

During the woman's absence, her tasks completed, Karen ventured from the kitchen and along to the main room where she observed the shotgun had been left propped by the front door. At

159

first a tempting sight, it occurred to her that she would have no idea how to use it and that Mrs Baxendale, having previously slipped the cartridges into the pocket of her apron, would probably have left the weapon unloaded. She returned to the kitchen only minutes before Mrs Baxendale entered through the utility room.

'Now there's things you need to know about so you can 'elp outside as well as int' 'ouse,' the woman announced after inspecting the result of Karen's labours. 'Follow me if you please.'

Karen was conducted from the house via the rear door, pausing to take up her allocated coat on the way. After the heat of the kitchen she was taken aback by the relative chill of the Pennine air and staring hard, noted how the windows of their car were covered in condensation. This was to be an instructional tour, one where Karen followed but said nothing during their time in the cowshed where a pair of bovines swayed, snorted and stamped, and where Mrs Baxendale explained the skills of milking. Twice she remarked, 'Ope you're takin' note, girl.' But Karen stared without seeing because her thoughts were elsewhere. Further time in the chicken coop had ended with a visit to the stone-walled vegetable garden, partly sheltered at one side by the cowshed and greenhouse built as a lean-to against it. It was when emerging from the greenhouse she spotted Richard returning from the quarry with Grimshaw ambling a short way behind. Her first impulse was to call out to him but Mrs Baxendale turned to her, saying, 'I've other things to be got on with now those two are back. You've seen where we keep the cows and you've seen the 'ens and 'ow they're fed so you'll 'ave a better idea of 'ow to go about it tomorrow when I'm busy with other things. Milkin't' cows we'll talk about again in good time because it 'as to be done twice a day and 'as to be done proper.'

Karen had taken little notice over much of Mrs Baxendale had said. She remained silent, her arms folded, her gaze averted. She would try her best to avoid doing what Mrs Baxendale would sooner or later insist upon. Whether the woman realised that or not seemed to make little difference as she added, 'So for now go about on your own where we've just been and think over in that pretty little 'ead of yours all of what I've explained. Stay clear of that outbuildin' over there if you know what's good for you 'cos that's where our Grimshaw lives and do not – I say do not go no further than where't geese are kept. They'll need to be fed from't vegetable peelin's – another job I'm sure you'll manage.'

What the woman had said confirmed her suspicions; it was to that tiny house, if house it really was, Grimshaw would retire at night. Allowed the opportunity to wander unsupervised, Karen wanted only to hurry toward Richard but Mrs Baxendale was already heading in that same direction. Karen stood watching Richard, calling to him in her thoughts, though he evidently had not seen her. A final glance confirmed the three were not returning to the house but would carry on past it, so she strode the short distance to the car, wiped condensation from a side window with her sleeve and peered through in hope of seeing the keys. The

161

keys, of course, were not there and it came as no surprise when she discovered the doors were locked. She stepped back toward the greenhouse then paused to glance up at the sky. High above, in a broad patch of open sky, was something that normally would pass unnoticed and elicit no comment, a vapour trail, and directly ahead of it the glinting mote of a jet airliner. Karen stared hard at it, almost tempted to wave and wanting to shout, to yell aloud, 'Hey – look down here! Help us! Please come and help us!' but that distant image of impossible hope soon disappeared from sight behind a grey cloud.

Amid the cluster of outbuildings there was one Mrs Baxendale had not referred to when they had earlier passed by it. Karen determined to look inside for no other reason than, like much else, it might offer some clue to their means of salvation. Glancing about she unlatched, pulled open the creaking wooden door and slipped inside. The single large window looked out not onto open land but revealed little more than the stone wall of the outbuilding occupied by Grimshaw, and a part of the greenhouse. A heavy odour permeated the still silence. Cheese.

By a solid old table at the centre of the room, stood a wooden vat or churn. Close by it rested a number of small wooden casks and a rustic three-legged stool. She concluded Mrs Baxendale must actually make cheese here, or until recently had. Over against the wall to her left ran several wooden cupboards. Stepping across, Karen reached out and opened the first of them to find it contained boxes of safety matches and white candles, as did the second. The third cupboard was, to her surprise, filled with more bars of soap and other mundane kitchen items she took little time to examine. In the fourth and largest were stacked several hard-rind cheeses, some covered with green mould. Karen wondered briefly if Mrs Baxendale planned to involve her in the process of cheese making because cheese appeared to be an important part of their frugal menu. She wondered also why the cheeses were contained within the cupboard. Were there rats here and could they somehow get into this and other buildings? Did rats eat cheese? She had little idea what rats might or might not prefer on their menu but knew only that she loathed the creatures. She returned to the first drawer and again looked down at the matches. There appeared to be twenty or thirty larger sized boxes. Even so, even with those contained in the second drawer and possibly more somewhere in the kitchen, these must be a finite and therefore a precious commodity. There were nevertheless plenty here, so glancing aside at the door, she slipped one of the boxes into the pocket of her apron.

Karen stepped from the outbuilding and peered about but could see or hear no one. She thought about the track leading away from the far side of the house and questions pirouetted through her head. Could she possibly get to the track without being seen? Was there another way to it via the rear of the house? How long would it take to hurry along the track, across the clearing and to the side road? How long then to reach the main road? How long before

163

she could phone the police, or if her mobile phone still did not work, stop a passing vehicle for help? Then how long before Mrs Baxendale would realise she had fled? She was uncertain as to whether or not she could make it to the main road but she truly believed that if she did escape then Mrs Baxendale would shoot Richard or have Grimshaw kill him. After all, the woman had made it chillingly clear - she had nothing to lose.

Karen continued on where she had walked earlier with Mrs Baxendale, stopping at the point beyond which she had been told not to go. There she stood to gaze across at the woods and at the rising hills beyond. Now she noticed, outside the allocated area, hardly further away from her than was the main house, another stone building, this quite plain and smaller even than a modest single garage. The building appeared intact. It attracted her attention partly because she had been told the area was out of bounds and partly because, forever hopeful, Karen again considered nothing ought to be overlooked. She was thinking how best to approach the building without being seen when a call from Mrs Baxendale summoned her back to the house. There she found herself once more in the utility room. 'Where's Richard?' she asked, slipping off the heavy coat.

'Back int' stable waitin' for the dinner you're about to cook,' came the terse reply, 'so best get on with it, girl, because I've other things to do. Aye, and just you remember, peelin's and other food scraps goes to the chickens 'an geese.'

Karen saw there was nothing to be gained at present other than by doing as she was told. The woodstove was hot, its fire glowing beneath. Mrs Baxendale left her alone so Karen, in faded cotton apron, set about the hated task of peeling potatoes, rinsing vegetables in cold water, dismembering and slicing raw chicken, this last an unpleasant task she remembered helping her mother with. In time she had water boiling in copper pans and chicken roasting in the side oven.

She was wrapping a dishcloth around the hot handle of a pan when the window to the left of the stove darkened. She looked up to see that grotesquely disfigured face bearing the hideous grin that seemed forever set upon it. Grimshaw continued to stare at her, one hand pressed against the glass, saliva glistening at the side of his face where the shattered-teeth and jawbone were part exposed. Karen shrank back in horror, closed her eyes and turned away shaking uncontrollably, chilled despite the heat of the kitchen. When she opened her eyes Grimshaw had gone but for several heartbeats she dared not move. The sound of bubbling water in the pans demanded she return to her work and she resumed wrapping the cloth about the pan handle. Directly to her right she became aware of the outer door opening – the very door to the rear of the house that previously had been locked. The inner door to the kitchen was slightly ajar but through the steam-hazed glass his ominous form loomed large. Then larger still. The door swung open and, stooping to avoid the lintel, Grimshaw entered. Able now to stand fully upright

165

he stared hard at her, steel grey eyes gleaming above that bizarre parody of a perverted Greek comedy mask. 'Ahhh, p-pretty lady,' he breathed.

Eyes wide with fear, Karen gripped the heavy pan. 'Get away from me!' she cried but Grimshaw moved fully into the kitchen repeating in a slow, laboured growl, 'Ahhh, yes, p-pretty lady – p-pretty lady.' He raised a soiled hand toward her. Karen backed away, her arms aching mercilessly with the weight of the pan then she felt the closed door to the hallway against her shoulder and could go no further. He must not touch her - no he must not! But Grimshaw stepped closer. He made a sudden grab at the collar of her dress as she tried to turn away but missed and seized the chain of the locket which he wrenched from her neck. Karen swung the pan aside and was about to dash its contents into his face when a voice from behind called, 'Grimshaw – leave the girl alone! Leave 'er I said and get thaself out of the kitchen!'

Grimshaw hesitated, looking from one to the other, seeming to tower over the slight figure of Mrs Baxendale so that Karen feared he might sweep her aside with a stroke of his arm. 'Oh, right, Ma,' he drooled, backing slowly away, 'leave 'er alone now. Y-yes.' Karen, no longer able to support the pan, stumbled about to let it down with a resounding clang upon the hot stove where water splashed over the side to billow up a loudly hissing, expanding cloud of steam. But Grimshaw still had the locket prancing from his fingers and Karen, turning to face him yelled, 'Give me that! Give it back, now!'

166

'Give it back to 'er, there's a good lad,' urged Mrs Baxendale, sternly, as she stood before him. Grimshaw peered down at her then at the locket and meekly held it out on the palm of his hand. Karen stepped quickly by the woman, reached to snatch the locket from him then returned to the hallway door where she stood ready to flee. 'Now go back to your nice 'ouse and rest a while,' continued Mrs Baxendale in what struck Karen even in those terrifying moments as a surprisingly amiable manner. 'Go on, lad. Go on and Ma will bring your nice dinner over soon.'

Like an admonished child Grimshaw lowered his gaze and mumbled, 'Y-yes, Ma, I'll g-go to my 'ouse now.' He backed out of the kitchen but his gaze was still upon Karen as he shuffled through, head bowed, to the outer door.

Clutching the broken chain of her locket, Karen, shaking uncontrollably, watched Mrs Baxendale follow close behind him to secure the outer door. As she re-entered the kitchen Karen blurted, 'Keep that – that bloody, whatever you want to call him, away from me!'

'I'll talk to 'im, girl, aye, I'll do that,' she responded tersely, 'and I'll not forget to relock the outer door next time. But understand – though he can't think too well 'e's still a man and, God forgive 'im, still craves the ways of the flesh.'

'What?' responded Karen, blazing angrily. 'You're telling *me* to understand! I'll tell you what I understand. I understand that *you* are keeping us here as prisoners. You have to let us go because this cannot continue any longer! Can't you see that!'

Mrs Baxendale's response was ominously calm and measured: 'Our Grimshaw's out of the way now so you can carry on as you were. If you see 'im by chance close by again an' I'm not around, go up to the room where your stuff is and wait. He knows 'e's never to go up there and never 'as.' She moved back a pace and peered down at what Karen was holding. 'My gran'mother 'ad a locket very like that,' she said as if what had occurred only minutes before was of little or no concern. 'Aye, very old it were. Let me 'ave a look.'

Mrs Baxendale held out her hand to take and inspect the locket but Karen ignored the gesture, thrust the locket down into her apron pocket, next to the box of matches, and turned away. 'Please thaself, girl,' the woman muttered. 'I'll be back 'ere in due course to see 'ow you're gettin' on.'

Unable to think clearly upon what Mrs Baxendale had been saying, she watched her unlock and open the outer door then pass through to relock it before setting off. Karen remained still, eyes closed until a degree of calmness reasserted. She reached to retrieve and examine the locket and broken chain. One of the delicate links was pulled open so she considered the chain should be easy to repair. She slipped it back into her apron and returned her attention to the pans, moving these aside to a cooler surface then looking about the kitchen. 'A small pair of pliers,' she muttered, 'that might fix the chain.'

Searching through the kitchen drawers she could find nothing of use although once again the knives appeared a very real temptation. Among the clutter she knew already there were six table knives together with six large and small spoons and six forks plus one bread knife and a large carving knife. If she concealed one of the table knives and took it with her to the stable that evening, would Mrs Baxendale notice it was missing? She decided the risk was too great and, reluctantly, closed the drawer.

Until now Karen had only opened those cupboards she had been obliged to access but opposite the stove there was the thin, tall cupboard none too obvious against the inner wall of an alcove where also were jammed a pair of moribund electric heaters, one balanced on top of the other, with towels hanging from a rail above. There had been no reason for her to open that particular cupboard. It was away from the rest and appeared to her as impractical except perhaps for the storage of tins and jars on its shelves. But here again curiosity took hold. She pulled open the door and sufficient light invaded the interior of the cupboard to reveal a now useless upright vacuum cleaner occupying less than half its depth. Shelves above bore a defunct toaster and other dust-gathering small electrical items. There seemed to be nothing of interest except that on the uppermost shelf, in the gloomy space close to the top of the cupboard there rested, almost unnoticed, another even less significant object. Karen was about to close the door when she hesitated, listened to the silence, glanced from side to side then reached up to take the object down. It proved to be a battered and faded dark green tin of a kind that might once have contained the pens and pencils belonging to a student. It evidently did contain something and as she lifted the tin, intending to replace it, a metallic rattling sounded from inside. Karen again checked to ensure there was no one close by, no one able to see her, then prised up the lid. She caught her breath, stood open-mouthed and gazed in heart-quickening silence with fingers poised above the opened tin.

***

Karen ate alone. Mrs Baxendale eventually returned accompanied by Grimshaw who remained at the front door. The woman collected a tray of food for Richard who waited confined within the stable but first she checked beneath the plate to satisfy herself that nothing had been concealed there. A little later she returned to gather up dishes of food for herself and Grimshaw but spoke not at all to Karen before leaving. After washing the dishes, which she placed to dry on the rack above the stove, Karen looked once more at the narrow cupboard and imagined that it possessed within that dark recess a glowing, beating heart of hope. She trod quietly from the kitchen and up to the bedroom. From her apron pocket she retrieved the tube of hand cream. Rubbing the cream into her hands she stared through the window at a lowering sky, her thoughts overwhelmed by what she had discovered a short time ago. Within an hour she would be taken from the house by Mrs Baxendale and Grimshaw to join Richard.

***

'Thank god you're all right,' Richard said as Karen eased herself down to the straw bed next to his.

'Yes, I suppose I am as long as she keeps that dreadful beast of a man away from me – but, Richard, I have to tell you I -.'

'Karen, let me tell you first,' he interrupted. 'I went out with her pet gorilla. We went over to the quarry and I saw the rock formation responsible for that wailing noise – you know, her divine voices. It happens when the wind blows through a kind of natural cavity. Anyhow, she's after me repairing the fence along the side of the quarry so I spent part of this afternoon sawing wood and chopping a couple of stakes with an axe. If he hadn't stood watching me from far enough away I swear I would have done for the bastard with that axe before he could land one on me with that spade of his. It sounds ridiculous if you think about it but I swear he knew that's what I had in mind. That old bitch walked by with her shotgun a couple of times as well. So, what about you – what've they threatened you into doing?'

'Please, Richard, I have to tell you something really, really important but there was something else happened earlier.'

'Something else - what d'you mean?'

'First promise you won't do anything stupid.'

'How can I promise anything until I know what you're going to say?'

'In the kitchen, Richard, he – Grimshaw, tried to – to -.'

Richard sat upright and demanded angrily. 'Tried to what?'

'He tried to grab hold of me in the kitchen then he - he broke the chain on my locket. He didn't do anything else because she turned up in time. I have to tell you because in the morning you'd have seen I wasn't wearing it and you'd have asked me why; I know you would.' She drew the locket and chain form the pocket of her apron and held it before him but in near darkness there was nothing he could make of it.

Richard eased back beside her, saying, 'Karen, we'll have to try and get away from here, whatever it takes, whatever the risk. Is there any chance you can smuggle a knife out of that kitchen – preferably a large one? A meat knife, maybe? If I can hide it in my coat, if I can get close enough to him then I swear I'll -.'

'I've thought about that, Richard, I really have, but I've seen her checking things. I'm certain she counts everything in those drawers. Most of the stuff in there wouldn't be much use anyway - not against that brute of a man. Don't anger either of them, whatever you do – please don't anger them!'

'I'm not stupid, Karen. I've no intention of confronting a retard that's built like a bloody tank or a mad woman with a shotgun unless I've some means of making a proper job of it. I'll find something - a spade, a brick – anything. First chance I get, I'll finish what her old man began when she isn't around. There's no alternative is there.'

'Richard – no! Listen to me, please - there's something far more important, all right? I found where she keeps the keys to our car.'

'You found the keys!' he exclaimed, twisting once more upright. 'Where are they? Have you got them with you?'

'No I haven't. I came across a tin containing a few old coins and some of her own keys. Ours were in there with them but I didn't want to take them away in case she found out. You and I are kept apart during the day so those keys are of no use to us unless we can get out of here together at night.'

'But why the hell would she keep them in the kitchen when she leaves you alone in there?'

'I don't know, Richard, but I'm telling you that's where they were – both of them. Maybe it's out of habit, you know, because she always kept things like that in there, or - or maybe she thinks that if I'm doing the cleaning upstairs I'd be searching for them in her room. It was pure chance that I -.'

'Karen, now listen.' he interrupted. 'Take those keys, get to the car and drive off when they're both shoving me back in here. I'll create a fuss and delay them. Maybe then I'll grab my chance and make a dash for it. Seeing those bottle bottom glasses of hers I have to wonder how good her aim is and I'll take a chance on outrunning her pet gorilla.'

'Richard, I can't!' she protested. 'If you're in here with them when I do that they could easily kill you; you know they could and we both know, don't we - they probably would.'

'Yes - fine, well I'll go back to the quarry in the morning with those stakes I cut and maybe there -. I thought this morning I might get him close to the edge. Maybe tomorrow I'll get the chance, but he's cunning I tell you, like an animal.'

Neither spoke for a while and the stable was in total darkness when Karen said, 'Richard – those keys.'

'Yes?'

'I mean, that tin with the keys in it – I'm wondering now if it was there because that's where her husband always kept it when he was alive. Some people do things like that, don't they? When someone close to them dies, they don't want to change anything. I managed to see inside her bedroom and -'

'You did what!' he exclaimed.

'Oh, I had time and it wasn't locked, and she knows I went in there. It was like a shrine with lots of mementoes and old photographs, as if nothing from outside had been added and nothing taken away in years. Yes, that's the way it looked. That could be why she didn't want our keys in there. They would have been an intrusion, no matter how small.'

Richard slipped an arm about her shoulder and kissed her cheek. 'Yes, maybe you're right, but you're talking about her as if she's an ordinary human being who deserved sympathy rather than a deranged old hag. And your locket – I mean the broken chain. If I get the chance then maybe I can fix it sometime tomorrow. There's a toolbox next to her generator and I saw a pair of pliers in it. If I can sneak in there and grab them I reckon I could squeeze the link shut easily enough. What d'you have hidden inside your locket? I think I asked you a while back, didn't I?'

'Yes, Richard, so you did,' replied Karen coolly as she slipped the locket and chain back into her apron, 'but I really bother worry about fixing it; we've a lot more than that to worry about, haven't we. Oh, and I came across other things in her utility room when she wasn't around: bars of soap and a drawer full of matches – there looked to be several dozen boxes. And candles – there must have been hundreds of them, and there are even more in one of the other buildings where it looks like she makes cheese. Her husband must have been getting them in after they agreed to leave the farm and stocking up before their deadline to quit. It's all smaller items so that might explain why she's run out of toilet rolls – you'd need lots of large boxes to collect enough of them - but then there wouldn't be anywhere to flush the paper would there.' Karen reached into her apron pocket, saying, 'I wondered if anything might be of use to us, that's all, so I er, I pinched a box of matches from the outhouse. I doubt if she counts those as well. What d'you think?'

'You mean like setting fire to the stable doors,' he remarked. 'Wouldn't I just love to; we could pile some of that straw against it and - but no, her damned geese might get started if she didn't see the flames first then the pair of 'em would be waiting outside before we could get clear, unless we choked to death first.'

'I suppose you're right, it would be too dangerous, but I could pinch a candle or two as well for us use in here.'

'I'd rather you didn't,' responded Richard. 'That would mean we were accepting the situation for days to come and if she found out, if she smelled the thing in the morning, I bet you'd be for it.'

'Just a thought,' sighed Karen. 'You're probably right.'

'Lots of candles,' Richard continued. 'D'you realise what that means? It means she was lying about that damned generator of hers. It must have already broken down before her old man died and he'd been no more able to repair the thing than I could. No wonder they got hold of so many bloody candles. But how about yesterday? You were going to tell me in fuller detail everything you learned about those two; you know, every little bit. So please, Karen, I really do need a complete picture as well as knowing what you think of it all.'

'Yes, Richard and I've been pondering on and off over what she said ever since. At the time I wasn't sure what to make of it but now I think it must all be true.'

Richard listened in silence as Karen related again the bizarre tale offered to her by Mrs Baxendale. After she had finished he declared, 'Brilliant! So she's pretty well given you her life story! Did she tell you what she did with her husband afterwards?'

'No, I – I don't know. She must have buried him somewhere, I suppose.'

'Maybe we ought to hang on here out of sympathy and help run the place as volunteers.' He stared angrily into darkness then added, 'No one should get away with what you've described - not any of this - not nowadays.'

'Grimshaw, or whatever his real name was,' Karen reflected, 'must have been an ordinary man doing his job before that happened to him.'

'Someone must surely have missed him when he didn't show up for work,' said Richard.

'Yes,' agreed Karen, 'and if he had a family there must be people still wondering what happened to him.'

'But she told you no one came here looking for him so it could be he wasn't a registered employee. Could be whoever took him on paid cash in hand with no questions asked so's to save themselves a few quid. Maybe he was hired just to find out who was getting in there and pinching their stuff. It's an expensive business employing people nowadays so maybe they didn't want the powers that be to know about him.'

'I suppose you're right,' she sighed. 'And now you've got me wondering what she did do with her husband after he died.'

'Perhaps he wasn't dead.' Richard commented. 'Perhaps he buggered off out of it when he saw what they'd done to Grimshaw but she doesn't want admit it. She lied about her generator after all. The woman is definitely mad! Yes - raving mad - concealing what happened to that man and holding us here.'

'Yes, perhaps she really is mad.'

177

'What d'you mean, perhaps!' he responded with rekindled anger. 'No one right in the head could do what she's done - tell me if I'm missing something. And what makes it worse is that she's a religious nut. She thinks some god or other is telling her to do what she's doing when the wind blows through those damned rocks. If only I could get my hands on that bloody shotgun of hers I'd -! Well I know what I'd do to him as an act of kindness, and you said you were ready to put a knife into her, didn't you?'

'Yes, it's the first time I've really felt I could do anything like that. Richard, there's no way I'd try to justify what she's done before or what she's doing now; of course I'm not. I'm simply trying to understand why she's doing it. I think it's her way of hanging on to what was always hers. Her life - her identity. She believed they were trying to take from her everything she and her husband had worked for and cherished. I think you know the effect that can have on people. Remember what you were telling me as we were leaving Manchester?'

'Well, more or less, but go on.'

'You were saying how people need to use their imagination and initiative and get on with things. Isn't that what she's done in her dreadfully misguided way? And what else did you say - there's a way around life's problems if you try? But she and her husband couldn't just shift over in society the way other people do because they were really never a part of it. This farm was their world. It's pretty well all she ever knew. She's a prisoner of her own past and for her there's no way out.'

178

'Well Karen, sweetheart, we're prisoners of her present but we *do* have to find a way out. And knowing why she's like she is sure doesn't make me feel any better.'

'No, Richard, nor me, but in your line of business, in financial dealings, you must have seen people lose everything through matters beyond their control.'

'That's right,' he replied, 'but as far as I'm aware none of 'em ever took to committing grievous bodily harm or kidnapping people.'

'Fine, Richard, but what I'm trying to say is – is perhaps we all ought to appreciate the effect our actions have on others. If everyone did, then maybe this wouldn't have happened to us. Can you be certain none of your own decisions haven't caused real harm to someone else?'

'No I can't be certain; in fact they quite possibly have, but so much in life is a risk and some of us have to make decisions one way or another. And as you imply, if we could predict what was likely to happen then we wouldn't be stuck in the back end of nowhere, locked in a cold stable, fed on a starvation diet and with our damned lives under threat from a madwoman with a shotgun and a retard who'd kill without a second thought! No, we'd be in some cosy little wine bar and you'd be looking as lovely as the first minute I spotted you. No, at times life isn't fair.' Richard lay back in the straw, closed his eyes and said, 'In a minute I'm going to wake up in the hotel, look at you and say, Christ, what a lousy dream I just had.'

Karen lay back and whispered, 'No, Richard, it isn't a dream. If only it was.'

Chapter 6

The morning was clear and the sky arrayed with tranquil cumulus when Richard set out pushing a small metal wheelbarrow. Contained within this was a roll of wire netting and two wooden stakes together with wire cutters, the hammer he had discovered in the toolbox where the generator was housed, and a packet of large metal staples. He was followed a few paces behind by the lumbering Grimshaw carrying spade and sledgehammer. The sledgehammer grasped in his right hand he swung as though it weighed little more than a straw broom.

They passed by the singing stones which that day, in calmer air, conveyed no message of destiny across the valley. Richard stopped two paces from the edge of the quarry, where the fence was broken. There he halted to wait and see what Grimshaw would do. Grimshaw eyed him steadily, stepped closer, lowered the sledgehammer to the ground and announced in a grumbling tone, 'You 'ave to d-do as Ma s-says. Fix th-the fence.' Then he backed slowly away.

Richard looked at the stakes, the netting roll and for seconds longer at the sledgehammer before moving closer to the edge. The shed at the bottom of the quarry was again within sight and its presence challenged him even more than it had the previous day. Now it was a goal to be attained simply because it was there, a relic of a saner world that had nothing at all to do with the farm or its deranged owner. Grimshaw stood watching him with the spade clasped horizontally. Richard placed the contents of the wheelbarrow onto the ground closer to the quarry edge then turned to the task in hand. He had to appear busy, he had to accomplish something so he picked up one of the posts. He had never before repaired a fence nor could he recall ever having seen anyone do so, but it was obvious enough that a new post should be hammered into the ground where an earlier one had stood. There was still evidence of a hole where the ground was softer but it appeared to Richard that the damage was not recent. He positioned the first stake into the hole and pushed down with his weight. He stepped back to see the stake bedded firmly enough to remain upright. His next move had to be employment of the sledgehammer. He stooped to raise this up, muttering, 'Oh, Christ,' when finding it weighed more than he expected even when wielded in both hands. Only too well did this serve to emphasise the advantage Grimshaw would have over most men, including Richard himself, in sheer physical strength. He raised the sledgehammer awkwardly and struck the post a cautious first blow, then a more confidant second and third. It required five more blows for him to consider the stake upright and sufficiently well founded. Lowering the sledgehammer to the ground with a whistle of breath he took up and was about to position the second post when he turned to observe Grimshaw had seated himself on the stone slab with the spade propped at his side. His hands rested on his lap and his head was tilted forward as if he had fallen asleep. Richard took a deep breath, lifted up the sledgehammer and stood to judge the distance between himself and Grimshaw. His heartbeat quickened. He took another breath, raised the sledgehammer chest high and in his thoughts, 'I'll have the bastard now! Yes – now!'

As if knowing his intentions Grimshaw leapt to his feet with startling agility, seized the spade and crouching low, approached Richard with a fierce, rumbling, 'Gahhh! Ma says b-bang you on 'ed if you don't b-be'ave. Y-you do what Ma says.'

'All right Mister Grimshaw, all right I'm doing it!' responded Richard, lowering the sledgehammer to the ground. Grimshaw advanced no further but maintained a threatening posture.

Richard mustered a broad smile and turned back to his allotted task as Grimshaw called again, 'Do what Ma says! Y-you do what Ma s-says!'

Richard collected up the second stake and stepped closer to the quarry edge but with his attention still diverted by Grimshaw he caught his foot against the roll of wire netting and fell sprawling. The post flew from his hands, rolled away and slipped over the edge. Gasping hard, appalled at having been so close to following the post down there to certain death, he scrambled backward until well clear. Grimshaw continued to watch with his mouth hanging wide. Richard, wondering what the man might do, struggled to his feet only to find Grimshaw staring at him in puzzled silence.

'Did you see that, Mister Grimshaw?' Richard called, thinking at once how some advantage might be gained from the mishap. 'Did you see what just happened? That spare post just fell all the way into the quarry! Now I'll have to go down there and get it! Do you understand?'

Still Grimshaw waited. Richard suspected, and certainly hoped, that the man was confused and incapable of dealing with the situation. 'See,' he continued, mustering a wider smile, 'I'll have to go down there and find the post – okay?'

Grimshaw still did not respond so Richard gestured again to the quarry. 'I have to bring that post back here so I can finish the job. If I can't do that then Ma will be very angry and you wouldn't like that would you Mr Grimshaw?' He gestured in the direction of the access route at the far end of the quarry though he realised that from where the man was standing it would not be visible. 'There's only one way in and out,' Richard continued, 'so I have to come back here, don't I - okay?'

Grimshaw rolled his head from side to side. 'M-ma says you 'aven't to g-go down there,' he growled. 'N-no, you 'aven't.'

'Then I can't finish the job can I, Mr Grimshaw, and Ma won't like that because it will be your fault for stopping me.' He moved closer to Grimshaw, his smile broadening further as he said, 'If you let me go down there to get the post back we can keep it secret, can't we? A secret between you and me and no one else – okay? A secret between you and me then Ma will never know.'

Eternal seconds clawed by, disturbed only by the call of circling crows, then Grimshaw responded with a contorted grin, 'Yeah, s-secret,' he drooled.

'Seeecret. Ma says you 'ave to d-do the job. Go an' b-bring the post back. Ahhh - our s-secret now.'

Richard set off slowly toward the spot where the fence switched to the right and Grimshaw, clutching his spade, followed some five or six paces behind, repeating now and again as he plodded along, 'Seeecret – s-seeecret.'

On reaching the angle where the fence turned, the quarry access was clearly visible to both and Richard, pointing to it, said, 'Now then, Mr Grimshaw, I have to climb right over this fence to find my way down that slope, see – that slope over there, and then I'll bring the post back. And don't forget, this will be our secret - just between you and me - yes?'

Grimshaw leered at him, said nothing, then raised and shook the spade in a gesture that Richard regarded as one of agreement, so he eased himself over the fence and continued along a short way before stopping to look back. With much relief he observed that Grimshaw had not followed him but stood watching from the other side of the fence. Away from the hill where the fence had terminated, the slope leading into the quarry was only a short, stumbling walk down to his left. Richard paused once more to check if Grimshaw had after all decided to follow. Perhaps afraid to approach the unwelcoming abyss, Grimshaw's menacing form remained silhouetted against the sky. Richard trudged on until turning to head down the slope. What had been an access route for heavy vehicles was now overgrown with weeds and clumps of grass. Less than halfway down the slope Richard ascertained that Grimshaw was no longer visible, which meant he must also be out of the other man's sight. Free of constant supervision, this would allow him more time to consider their situation in the clear light of day.

Unlike the rest of the quarry the side to his left, above which the fence ran, was not terraced back but soared as a precipitous limestone edifice from which bushes and small plants sprouted. Richard estimated the cliff must rise to well over a hundred metres high. This side was presently in shade but sunlight spilled down elsewhere to illuminate much of the quarry floor.

'I'll be lucky to find the damned thing down here,' he muttered. Alone and feeling overwhelmed by the scale of the place, he had almost reached the bottom of the slope and was thinking of Karen when his attention was caught by something further along than the shed; something close beneath the base of the cliff; an object conspicuous by its blue colour amid this vast arena of grey stone. High above the object, the gap in the fence he had begun to repair was just visible. As Richard walked on, avoiding pools of dark water, non-descript rusted equipment and rubble fallen from the cliff, he wondered how much time had passed since the calls of men and the clamour of machinery had echoed about those gaunt walls. Hesitating then turning to face the shed only a few steps to his right he muttered, 'I'll take a look in there first in case that big bastard decides to follow me down here.'

He reached the shed, peered back toward the slope and upward again but of Grimshaw there was still no sign. The shed evidenced signs of dilapidation, its single, begrimed window was cracked, some of its planking revealed the onset of decay and its corrugated iron roof was rusted. He reached the single door on the side facing away from the ramp and grasped the flaking metal handle. Corroded hinges squeaked in protest as he eased the door open. Richard was not surprised to find the shed contained only a few yellowed newspapers and empty drinks cans scattered about the wooden floor. As he stood looking about the confined space a passing gust caused the door to sigh shut. A profound silence descended all about. A feeling of peace and contentment closed about Richard as though he had been cast adrift from the dire situation he and Karen had found themselves in. Closing his eyes, he was taken by an irrational desire to loiter, to stand unmoving and to contemplate only the isolation, the stillness and his own being in this temple of tranquillity.

A minute, perhaps longer, had passed before this reverie was swept aside by a pressing sense of urgency. He bent to pick up one of the old newspapers. The date on it informed him the quarry had been closed for nearly four years. He let the paper fall to where it had lain and was about to leave the shed when he spotted something laying to one side of the door – something laying in a dark corner, something that might so very easily have been overlooked. He reached to push open the door, hesitated, stooped to pick the object up, examined it, tapped away the grit and breathed, 'Ah, what have we here – yes, what *do* we have here.'

That small item, long since discarded as worthless, was to Richard a find of momentous importance. He slipped the precious object carefully into the inner pocket of his coat then with a final glance around he stepped outside the shed and eased the door shut with reverential care. He closed it so because, quite irrationally, it seemed the right thing to do now that humble, abandoned shed had presented him with such a gift. Glancing up again to check that he remained unobserved, Richard carried on until close enough to identify the blue object further along beneath the high wall. It was not, as he had at first assumed, an abandoned piece of equipment but to his surprise appeared to be the shattered wreckage of a car. Laying between himself and the car he spotted the wooden fence post so he stepped aside to pick this up. He might then have turned to retrace his steps but curiosity had taken hold and so he continued further. The sight of the car, as he approached closer, gripped him with foreboding. A few steps on and his shoes crunched broken glass. Richard stooped to peer inside. He froze then staggered back. Beneath the grim walls, within the crushing loneliness of the quarry, the horror contained within that metal husk was revealed.

***

'Apart from clearin' up and seein' to the stove,' announced Mrs Baxendale after breakfast, 'there's nothin' much to do int' 'ouse until you 'ave to prepare lunch, then after that there's cleanin' down 'ere. While your fancy man is out mendin' the fence you'll 'appen want to go out back then outside for a bit of fresh air when you've finished int' kitchen. It's a nice enough day – not too chilly, no, not for this time of the year. Take note of what I showed you yesterday so you remember what 'as to be done next time. Aye, and while you're out there you can collect a basket of firewood fromt' storage by the cowshed. Basket for the wood is just inside the kitchen door an' that's unlocked for the time bein'. But go no further than where I told you last time an' make sure you remember that. You'll 'appen be tempted to run off somewhere but don't bother because even if my Grimshaw doesn't catch you, as 'e may well do if I call for 'im, there'll be another that'll suffer. Do I make myself clear?'

'Perfectly clear - as always,' Karen responded with a cold stare, 'and there's something else that's just as clear. Richard told me about that rock formation near the quarry: that's where your heavenly sounds are coming from. It's just the wind blowing through them – not the voice of any god. No one is telling you to hold Richard and me here as prisoners. No one at all. Do you hear me – no one at all!'

'I know about the singin' stones, girl, it's my ruddy land after all and I've lived 'ere all me life. But it's the Lord above sends those winds with their message and it's also a requiem for my Len, rest 'is soul.'

'That's ridiculous!' exclaimed Karen, 'It's no more than a natural sound. I can hear it. Richard can and so could anyone else!'

The woman moved menacingly closer, stared into Karen's face and growled angrily, 'Aye, well

189

let me tell thee, there's them that 'ears the word of God but doesn't listen and them that listens but doesn't 'ear - so keep your blasphemous opinions to y'self, girl, an' do as I said.'

With a gasp of frustration Karen hurried away, glad of the opportunity once again to be alone and knowing Grimshaw was not close by. Picking up the basket she stepped through the outer door at the rear of the house, hesitating as she passed by the car, seeing in her mind the keys she had earlier discovered and thinking, 'Richard – if you were with me right now. If only. I'd grab those keys and we'd get away from here before they could stop us.'

Walking on she was nevertheless chilled by thoughts of Grimshaw as she eyed the modest building where he was accommodated. She looked toward the route Richard would have taken and hoped she would see him return later that morning. She crossed to the cowshed, to the covered enclosure at its far side where freshly chopped timber was stored. There she placed as much wood into the basket as she considered not too heavy to carry back afterwards, then she placed it aside. Close to the cowshed lay the vegetable garden, the lean-to greenhouse, and after that the chicken coop. Beyond the chicken coop, beyond where the geese strutted and nodded, there stood that other building, the smaller stone, slate-roofed structure she had earlier observed. To Karen it appeared a more recent addition, not as time-mellowed as the rest of the farm. Behind it spread the ash trees with the land rising steeply some way further out. Why, she asked herself, had Mrs Baxendale insisted upon her not going so far? Karen was tempted to regard the twice-expressed prohibition almost as an invitation in disguise. A challenge, perhaps - but why?

She passed by the greenhouse, pausing a while to think, then by the chicken coop where she again stopped to watch the clucking, pecking antics of the birds. She peered up at the sky, seeing more vapour trails, then looked back in the direction of the main house. It took her little time to realise the small building that so fascinated her was in direct line with the cowshed and farmhouse so unless someone was watching from the upper floor of the house it could not be seen. The geese appeared to be plucking at grass and whatever else they could find and Karen wondered, if she walked close by slowly, would they create a commotion? She looked about once more then continued on. Her intrusion did not excite the geese; they simply ignored her or strutted aside grunting as she made her way cautiously around their domain. She reached uneven ground, where an occasional rock protruded through the grass; the half-buried jaw of some long dead giant was how Karen imagined them.

Closer to the building Karen noted the door was set at a right angle from her direction of approach but there was no window visible on the wall facing her. She reached the door, stood apprehensively before it, looked aside then stepped by to peer around the corner. Propped against the wall beneath a window was a motorcycle, obviously abandoned some time ago and part concealed by a grey plastic cover. Only fleetingly did she wonder why it had been left there before returning her attention to the door where she observed there were two iron bolts but no locks. She had seen no locks on any of the other buildings except those about the main house and, of course, the stable had its sliding bar. At first assuming they may not have been used for some time Karen found the bolts slipped aside with little effort. With yet another sideways glance, she pulled the door ajar only to be met by an odd, cloying odour. She opened the door further. The odour was stronger. She hesitated then stepped cautiously inside but because the odour was now distinctly unpleasant she risked leaving the door slightly open. Light fell about the small interior from the single window on her left that allowed sight of the ash trees and hills. The space was part occupied by a bulky, odd-shaped form covered by sacking that took up more than a quarter of the floor area. Standing to the left of this, beneath the window, was a small, plain square table upon which rested an old-fashioned rosewood pipe with next to it a well-worn, dark leather tobacco pouch. The pipe and pouch were similar to those she recalled seeing her grandfather use in her childhood days. On the wooden floor by the table stood a brightly coloured ornamental vase containing wildflowers that looked to be no more than a few days old. Karen wondered at their presence. But the sacking; did it cover some kind of fertiliser or animal feed? Could that account for the smell? That frequently quoted but all too often ignored inner voice warned her to leave but she did not because curiosity, as with the tin in the utility room cupboard, might reveal something of advantage. Karen moved forward until the object was less than an arm's length away. She reached out slowly to tug on one corner of the sacking but had hardly touched it when it shuddered and slithered downward.

'Ohhh – oh god!' she cried, staggering back, gasping uncontrollably with hands clutching her face. Revealed to the waist, the corpse, its cracked parchment skin shrunk over protruding cranial bones, was seated in an ornately carved and cushioned wooden chair. Sparse grey hair clung about the sides of a skull, the teeth of which protruded from the retracted flesh of a mouth agape in the manner of a silent, raging scream. Its claw-like hands rested on the chair arms as though they might at any moment stir, begin to twitch and reach out to her. As she stared in numbed horror, one of the eye sockets glinted life and unable for the moment to move or utter another sound, Karen felt her very sanity cast adrift. From beside the shrunken eyeball emerged a shining black beetle. It crawled leisurely across the cheek then downward to vanish behind the collar of the sagging donkey jacket draped loosely about its near skeletal owner. Karen tottered back to the doorway but as she continued to stare, the sack slid all the way to its feet and the rotted abomination appeared about to rise quivering from its chair.

'Ohhh – oh, god!' wailed Karen once more as pressing a hand over her mouth she lurched into glaring daylight. She slammed the door shut, managing, only just, to slide back the bolts with shaking hands. She turned to lean against the timbers, breathing fitfully, almost choking, eyes closed tight as she tried to purge from her mind the scene she had witnessed. When her breath at last eased she looked across at the main house. Fearing Mrs Baxendale might have observed her, Karen made her way, trembling uncontrollably, back to the cowshed. There, head bowed, she leaned against the side facing away from the house, close to the basket of chopped wood she had earlier placed there. A little calmer now but feeling very cold, she looked at her watch to see the time approaching eleven-thirty. Another half hour would pass before the woman expected her to return with the wood, light the stove and begin preparing lunch. By then Richard might have returned, or perhaps he already had. She was desperate to be with Richard – desperate to inform him of the hideous object she had quite literally uncovered, desperate to hear his voice and to feel his arms about her.

**

In those thirty minutes since that shocking discovery she had wandered to the vegetable garden then entered the warm and reassuring sanctuary of the greenhouse to clarify her thoughts. She stared out to the surrounding hills and hoped to muster a degree of outward normality before facing Mrs Baxendale. Attempting to concentrate on other things, she observed how abundantly stocked and well ordered the greenhouse was and realised that to the woman she so feared and despised it must be a source of satisfaction as well as a time-consuming necessity. When her watch indicated the approach of midday Karen left the greenhouse but her anxiety and the macabre image she had witnessed that

194

morning returned in full measure as she walked back to the cowshed where she collected the basket of wood. She continued on to the house and approached the rear door, but as she raised a hand to open it the door sprang abruptly inward.

'Back 'ere now are you, girl,' said Mrs Baxendale. Her words were calm but behind them simmered thinly veiled sarcasm.

'It would appear so,' was Karen's terse response.

'Lookin' very pale, aren't we, girl. Not feelin' too well – is that it?'

'It's chilly out there,' Karen replied, 'and this basket is heavy, that's all.'

'Oh, chilly out there is it, so that's why y'look as if you've seen a ghost. Well maybe you 'ave seen one, or maybe it were somethin' very like that. I looked out from upstairs to see what you were about an' I saw you walkin' back towards the chickens. You went to that place over near yon trees when I said to keep away. You looked inside there, didn't you and I know what you saw! Na then, girl – admit it!'

Karen stared at her open-mouthed then turned aside, unwilling for the moment to respond.

'I knew you 'ad,' the woman continued. 'I could tell when you came back 'ere white as a sheet. You saw my Len!'

'How could you!' exclaimed Karen, twisting about to face her once more. Shaking her head she pushed hard past Mrs Baxendale and stepped through to the kitchen where she let fall the basket of wood before turning again. 'How could you leave him like that – your own husband? How?'

Mrs Baxendale followed and addressed her face-to-face once more. 'It were unavoidable, that's why!' she snapped. 'What wi' nursin' Grimshaw an' work about the farm I 'ad no time to bury 'is body and even if I'd 'ad time the ground is too thin and 'ard to dig deep enough. It seemed better to let 'im sit there in peace and in peace 'e must be left.' A grim smile crossed her face. 'My Len built that little retreat with 'elp from the men that used to work 'ere in past years. He used to take 'is pipe an' newspaper in there for a bit of peace an' quiet when't work were over. Now it's 'is final restin' place, an' that's where 'e'll stay so don't you stick your nose in there anymore!'

'It's appalling!' cried Karen, moving away to confront her from the other end of the kitchen. 'It's unforgivable! All the preaching - all this rubbish about hearing the voice of God and you've left your own husband's body to rot in that chair! Yes, and you wanted me to see it, didn't you! I know full well you did because you wanted to scare the shit out of me! And look what you and that - that whatever you want to call him have done to Richard and me! Well, you nasty old bitch, you'll be found out very soon - I know you will!' Karen hurried into main room but the woman followed her. Mrs Baxendale's severe gaze pierced Karen through as she hissed, 'Words, lass – ruddy words! Words comes easy to some folk but they won't do no 'arm to me. No!' She moved around the dining table toward visibly shaking Karen. 'We 'ave to do as we

196

are called to do and do it as we best can. And you'll learn to do as you're told you damned little 'eathen 'ussy! And you'll not raise your voice like that again and use profane language within these walls.'

Her move was sudden. Her arm swung up and the open-claw hand caught Karen a sharp blow across the cheek. Karen reeled back, clutching her face and hearing the voice penetrate as a hot knife through the turmoil of her own thoughts. 'Tha'll not mess wi' me, lass! These 'ands 'ave worked this farm. Aye, worked it 'ard as any man's. They're strong! I'm strong! A lot stronger than the prissy likes of thee so I won't need poor Grimshaw to keep you in *your* place - oh, no. Give me any more trouble, girl, and I'll give thee trouble and worse. Aye, any more nonsense an' you'll be confined upstairs at night an' not see your fancy man at all! Now get int' kitchen – there's plenty 'as to be done today because tomorrow is the Sabbath. Int' mornin' your man can chop more wood, you'll see to the kitchen then come lunchtime we will all gather to 'ear words from the Good Book.'

'And where,' demanded Karen, glaring at her, 'in your so-called good book, does it say you have the right to detain, torment and threaten innocent people? Tell me *that*!'

'It says,' the woman responded, 'that we all should 'eed the word of God and then his message will become clear. Whent' generator were workin' we 'ad Sunday service ont' wireless as well but nowt can serve us better than the Bible itself.'

Her cheek stinging, Karen looked on icily, trying to ignore her words as Mrs Baxendale

197

explained more about the planned Sunday reading. Karen offered no response as she stepped past Mrs Baxendale and returned to the kitchen. There she was determined to lose herself in the tasks that lay ahead, determined to think of nothing else until such time as the evening meals were dealt with. Then she would be allowed to re-join Richard in the place of confinement she almost regarded now as a refuge from the insane situation into which they had been precipitated.

***

Late afternoon had arrived and with the sun vanished below the hills Karen had already contrived enough food on the woodstove for Richard. While she had a little earlier been confined to the upstairs room, Richard had been allowed to use the utility room and kitchen, and doubtless would soon be returned to the stable. With potatoes, cauliflower and peas from garden, greenhouse and store cupboard bobbing in pans of water, and fried eggs sizzling, she was struggling to prepare three more meals when Grimshaw appeared at the window. Once again was that obscene, leering grin as he pushed close to the glass. The green curtain hooked to one side of the frame was within Karen's reach but to pull it across meant she would have to lean closer to the window and reach out with her fingers close to his face. She moved aside, cold with fear and tried to ignore Grimshaw's threatening image but seconds later he was gone. She reached to jerk the curtain over the window but withdrew her hand on realising that in doing so it would reduce further what little light there was from outside.

She had returned her attention to the woodstove when a darkening of the door to her right caused her to look about. Grimshaw had entered the utility room in silence and now was staring at her through the misted glass of the kitchen door. Mrs Baxendale had again left the outer door unlocked. Karen spun about, wrenched open a drawer and seized the meat knife, muttering, 'She's done it on purpose.' Then louder, 'That bloody bitch – she's done this on purpose!'

As she stood, chilled by fear, Grimshaw was turning and rattling the handle but the door into the kitchen was either locked or jammed. He pushed hard against the door, shaking then banging it violently with the palm if his hand as if he intended to break it down. Soon the glass had to shatter, perhaps the timbers also. Karen gripped the knife harder, then to her immense relief Mrs Baxendale appeared behind him. She placed a hand on his shoulder, uttered a few words and ushered him away with only a passing, expressionless glance at Karen and at the knife she held. Karen continued to grip the knife, waiting, listening until the two figures, vaguely discernible through the glass of the door, could no longer be seen and the outer door was locked.

She had already eaten and was washing her hands in tepid water when an hour later Mrs Baxendale reappeared in the utility room. She locked the outer door then unlocked the kitchen door to ask in a matter-of-fact manner, 'Is food ready for me ant' lad?'

'It's there,' replied Karen, gesturing to the stove then tuning to face her. 'You let him in again didn't you. You did it on purpose to scare me – I know you did.'

'It were an oversight, girl – no more than that and I were close by alt' time.'

'I want to get back to Richard now,' Karen demanded.

'Aye, tha can,' the woman assured her as Grimshaw loomed once more outside the kitchen window. Karen glanced at him and declared, 'You have to keep him away from me, do you understand! Just - just keep him away or I swear to you I'll use that knife - yes I will, no matter what happens!'

'Tha shouldn't be such a magnet t'men,' replied Mrs Baxendale, dismissively. 'Poor lad can't 'elp 'imself. Still, 'appen I ought to deal with it as best I can. As for now, we'll see you to the stable.

They left the house and approached the stable, Mrs Baxendale cradling the shotgun and Grimshaw following. Karen avoided looking at him but more than once she heard him growl, 'P-pretty lady.' When the stable door was opened Richard stood there waiting, arms folded in a gesture of defiance. Grimshaw grinned at him, raised a hand to his twisted mouth and drooled, 'S-seeecret.'

The remark of course meant nothing to Karen but Mrs Baxendale glanced questioningly at him then asked Richard, 'Is that fence repaired?'

'Best as I can do it,' responded Richard

As the doors closed against the diminishing light of day, as the iron bar grated, Karen and Richard faced each other with each anxious to speak first.

Karen gasped, 'Richard you wouldn't believe what I -.'

At the same time, Richard, in grave manner, began, 'Karen, love, I went down into the quarry today and -.'

Both stopped talking, each waited for the other to resume then Richard said, 'Let's sit down while we can still see what we're about then you'd better say what you have to say first.'

They sat together on the straw beds as Karen began, 'Richard I've seen her husband and -.'

'You've what! I thought the man was dead. Didn't she tell you he was?'

'Please listen to me – please, Richard, that's what I'm trying to tell you; I've seen him, or what's left of him. She keeps his body in that outhouse over near the trees. She's – she has him sat in a chair. It's as if he's waiting for her. She - she takes him flowers and - oh, god, it was dreadful – just utterly dreadful! And she knows I went in there and what I saw. And that retarded creature of hers – he tried to get at me again when I was in the kitchen. He seemed to come from nowhere; I didn't hear a thing until he was right at the kitchen door. Richard, I don't know how much more of this I can take. What with him prowling about and me seeing her dead husband in that chair, I'll end up mad as her. Look, honestly, this has to end soon whatever the risks we face.'

'Her husband - that's, well - that's incredible.'
He thought for a while on all Karen had told him
then continued, 'and so is what I saw this morning,
and it isn't going to help cheer you up any.'

'Wh-what d'you mean?' she asked, squeezing
the hand he reached out to her.

'I was trying to fix that fence above the quarry
but I tripped and fell. One of the posts rolled over
the edge and I – god, I nearly went over myself. I
convinced the ogre I had to go down there to bring
the post back. He saw things my way and
fortunately he didn't want to follow me. Anyway,
once I was out of his sight it gave me the chance to
see if there was anything that might be of use to us
and I wanted to take a look inside the shed. I found
something in there that – no, I'll come back to it in a
minute. That gap in the fence – it was caused
because a car had gone through. I found the remains
of it smashed up at the bottom of the quarry.
There's no way it could be seen from the top on this
side and no one on the far side could possibly make
much of it. I walked over to take a closer look and –
Karen, love, there were two bodies in there - two
people crushed inside the wreckage.'

'Two people in the -. Oh, Richard, what are you
saying?'

'I'm saying that car must have been driven or
pushed through the fence with them inside it. How
long ago I wouldn't care to guess at but they must
have been down there quite some time because they
were – well, the bugs and the birds must have been
at work. I couldn't make out whether they were

male or female and I – I couldn't stand there looking at them any longer.'

Neither spoke for a time then Karen asked, 'But why, Richard, why do you think -?'

Richard took a deep breath. 'They either drove over the edge at night trying to get away from those two, which I doubt because the ground is too rough for a car, or – or they were pushed over. I guess her pet gorilla could have done it and that's what I think must have happened.'

'But why?' Karen asked. 'And you're saying they were murdered, aren't you? I mean, they – they must have been, otherwise why would -?'

'I don't know and I'm not sure I want to,' he replied. 'Perhaps they were older people, maybe too old to be of any use to them. Or maybe there was some other reason. But that nasty bloody woman is determined to keep her secret, whatever the cost.'

'I know what that other reason might be now I think about it,' breathed Karen. 'I remember the area well enough. It'll be getting a lot colder outside and here in this stable as the weeks go by. Not that it will matter too much to her I don't suppose.'

'What d'you mean, it won't matter?'

'What I mean is *we* won't matter,' answered Karen. 'We'll still be needing food, her food, but there won't be enough work for us to do. She wants her life made easier for the time being but then -.' Don't you see, Richard, we'll be a liability.'

'Fine, I hear what you're saying; they've killed before so they'll kill again. They'll deal with us the way they did with those poor buggers down there in the quarry. She'll take it as God's will and use her bloody shotgun or - or get Grimshaw to do it. He'll only need a few words from her, I'm sure of that, and I doubt when it comes to it, it'll mean any more to him than chopping wood for the fire.'

'Richard, it's already mid-September. Winter's not so far away, especially here in the Pennines, so they *will* kill us unless we –.'

'Unless we get away sooner rather than later, and that's exactly what I'm coming to. Karen, I found this in the shed.'

Karen peered down in fading light at the object Richard had produced from his coat pocket. It was a lightly rusted hacksaw blade, one end of which was broken away. What remained appeared to be some twenty-five centimetres long.

'I've already tested it out,' said Richard. 'I can slip it between the doors and reach the bar outside but I guess it's not going to be easy. It'll take a long time but I'll have a damned good go at sawing through that bar so we can get out of here.'

'Oh, Richard,' she sighed, closing her eyes, 'so we have a chance at last.'

'Our only chance Karen, love, but we'll need those car keys. You have to get them before you leave the house tomorrow evening.'

'Okay but if I'm not able to, if she's watching me, we can still make a run for it and keep going until we reach the road - can't we? We know which way the track goes even if it's dark.'

'No, we mustn't risk that. We'd have to pass close to the house, and if those bloody geese started squawking she'd be out with her shotgun and he'd be after us - and I bet he'd catch one of us before we could get anywhere near the side road, let alone the main road. She'll probably be up and about before sunrise but who knows, he could be wandering around the place during the night the way he seems to have been when I wandered over here for help. If we can get to the car I reckon we've a far better chance. One problem, possibly – you heard him saying, "Secret" didn't you. She'd told him not to let me enter the quarry so I talked him into keeping it a secret. He kept on repeating the word when we got back, didn't he, and if he starts saying it in front of her then she might persuade him to spill the beans.'

'But, Richard, Grimshaw would have known the car was down there and would have known you'd see it – wouldn't he? I mean, if she'd had him push it over the edge after they'd -.'

'He might have if all the cogwheels in his head were connected,' cut in Richard, 'but luckily they aren't. It's probably escaped from his mind like so much else. The kindest thing for that poor sod would be a bullet in what's left of his brain.'

'Does it really matter if he tells her,' Karen asked. 'She won't know anything about the saw blade.'

'It could matter quite a lot. If she thinks we know about the car and the bodies she'll realise how much more desperate we are to get away. She might decide you and I have already passed our sell-by dates - then what.'

'Oh, god, yes, and talking of which, she's somehow worked out that it's Sunday tomorrow so after you've chopped more wood for her stove and

I've finished in her kitchen, we're to get a lunchtime Bible reading.'

'A what!' he exclaimed. 'You must be joking!'

'I'm not joking, Richard; we have to sit and listen to her preaching and that will include Grimshaw.'

'Oh, really – I can't wait. So after her damned sermon you should be able to get hold of those keys. D'you think you can do that?'

'I have to, don't I if we're to have any chance of getting away from here,' she replied, letting go of his hand as each lay back on their straw mattress.

'You definitely have to,' he confirmed, 'and I'll need a cloth to wrap around the blade. I don't think my handkerchief will be enough.'

'I'll get a cloth as well; that's the easy bit. At least I already have my shoulder bag with my cash and cards - but I'm not sure about getting my holdall or my suit. If she sees me with those she most certainly will be suspicious. I could try to get them downstairs during the afternoon when she's away from the house, as long as he's not around either. I could leave them behind the car where she won't notice then I'd need to get back to the kitchen. I expect she'll want an evening meal conjured up even on her precious Sabbath.'

'Better if you forget about the holdall and suit,' said Richard. 'I mean it - they're not worth the risk if we're talking mostly about clothes. My jacket is draped over the partition so I have my cash and cards same as you. My case is already with us, you have your mobile phone and with a bit of luck mine will still be in the car. Once we get far enough away from here we should be able to pick up a signal and call the police.'

'Then there's nothing else we can do, is there, but I'd rather not think any more about it - not right now.'

'You should try and get some sleep, me as well.'

'I - I don't know if I can. I'm really on edge and more so now it's dark. After what I saw in that outhouse and after what you told me about that car in the quarry I'm afraid to sleep in case it all comes back in the night. Really, I've never felt so scared or so bloody agitated.'

'Karen, I understand, yes, but you ought to try; we'll both need our wits about us tomorrow and we'll not get any sleep the next night.' It was too dark to see but he sensed her running fingers over the locket and realised how much comfort it must give her. 'That locket of yours,' he asked, 'is it a memento – does it have a photo inside of someone you were once close to, or someone you still are?'

Karen was silent for some moments then sat up again. 'Yes,' she responded angrily, 'that's the one thing you've been itching to find out about isn't it, Richard – the same as that bloody woman has!'

'Look, I'm sorry; there's no need to get upset, okay. I only -.' He thought from the sound of her voice she might be on the verge of tears and knew he must say nothing more on the subject.

'Having this, Richard,' she informed him after another pause, 'having this has helped me keep sane since we ended up in this madhouse! If that hag of a woman or that - that dreadful man tries to take it away they'll have to kill me! That's what – they'll have to kill me!'

'Karen, love, I wasn't trying to pry, I was just curious for the sake of it and nothing more. It really doesn't matter. Look, we're both so on edge and -.'

'Well, Richard, it *does* matter because you'd have found out sooner or later anyway – probably sooner. So in case you think it has anything to do with another man I can tell you right now it doesn't. No - it's a woman, Richard - another woman! All right?'

'Karen, there's no need to say anything about - .'

'And as for my work in the South of France, as for what we do, me and the rest of the girls that is – you'll find that even more interesting. We entertain the wealthy – some of them very much like you, Richard - people who can afford to sample what's on offer; people who can afford to indulge their sexual fantasies in full and I tell you it doesn't come cheap, if you'll pardon the pun.' She sank back into the straw and took a deep breath. 'There - now you know - I'm a high-class whore if you want to look at it that way. I fuck with men and women and most of the time I don't mind which. But then I dare say what I do is no worse than what you do. At least they get their money's worth out of me and the other girls I work with. Oh, I once felt guilty about it all; yes at first I really did but I soon got over all that - believe me I did.' A further silence, then, 'Maybe you thought I was an easy pull, Richard, sitting there on my own in that wine bar and hoping a man would drop by. Well maybe it was the other

208

way around. Maybe I saw you had plenty of cash and hoped you were willing to give me a good time when I had little else to do. I'm used to manipulating men, Richard. In fact women like me can get most men to do anything even when they think they're the ones in charge.' She gave a long sigh and added, 'It's an incentive for us to try a bit harder and get ourselves out of here isn't it since we both miss the good life. God, if the girls I work with could see the situation I'm in now they'd - no, I can't imagine what they'd think.'

For a time Richard said nothing. When he did speak, it was almost a whisper. 'Karen, love, I really don't give a damn what you do; I'm no self-appointed moralist. As you implied, I wouldn't be doing what I have been these past years if I was. But I do care about you. I care just the same as I did before you spoke out and right now I tell you, nothing is going change that. I'll try my damnedest tomorrow night to get us out of this rat-hole and back to civilisation and I'll do whatever it takes to avoid you being hurt in the process. As for me seeing you as an easy pull – well, I don't think you believe that. I – honestly, I was amazed when you agreed to have dinner with me.'

After further pensive seconds Karen reached for his hand once more. 'Richard, I'm really sorry for the way I spoke to you; you're the last person I should be taking it out on. It's not your fault we're in this situation; it's a one in ten million mischance, or fate if that's the way you see it. God, don't we so easily take life for granted when things are running the way we want.'

'Don't we just. What wouldn't I give right now for a hot shower, a good dinner and a half decent bottle of wine. No, a roadside café and a bacon sandwich would do just as well.'

'And a shave,' she said. From the sound of her voice he knew she was smiling as she added, 'You haven't shaved since we left Manchester. Your face is all stubbly and rough.'

'No, I decided I wouldn't be shaving again until we're out of here even if my electric shaver is still fully charged - and I wasn't going to use that old stuff of her husband's either. So there's an additional challenge; I have no intention of growing a beard so we have to get ourselves out of here before I do.'

'You know,' she sighed, 'I always worried about getting the right kind of conditioner for my hair and the right brand of eye liner. Now I treasure those moist tissues and that tube of hand cream in my bag like some people might a Fabergé egg. We might be trying our best to stay human but I already feel like one of her animals.'

They lay once more without speaking and stared into dark emptiness, then Karen said, 'Oh, well, now I've let off a bit of steam perhaps I will try to sleep, unless you – I mean, even here.' She squeezed his hand hard, she moved closer and Richard sensed how very much her mood had changed during those few moments of silence.

'Yes, Karen,' he breathed, 'yes, love, even here,' turning to kiss her and feeling in her breath a furnace of sensuality on his rough cheek. 'And let's make sure it's not the last time.'

Chapter 7

'Know ye not that the unrighteous shall not inherit the kingdom of God? Be not deceived: neither fornicators, nor idolaters, nor adulterers, nor effeminate, nor abusers of themselves with mankind. Nor thieves, nor covetous, nor drunkards, nor revilers, nor extortioners, shall inherit the kingdom of God.'

'Don't forget murderers and kidnappers,' muttered Richard as Mrs. Baxendale continued. 'And such were some of you: but ye are washed, but ye are sanctified, but ye are justified in the name of the Lord Jesus, and by the Spirit of our God.'

There were four seated at Mrs. Baxendale's lunchtime table. Karen and Richard were side-by-side, Mrs. Baxendale faced Karen and opposite Richard rested the bulk of Grimshaw. Before each of them was set out the result of Karen's enforced toil in the kitchen; bread, boiled eggs, roasted chicken legs and vegetables together with a glass each of cold water from the pump.

Mrs. Baxendale, had she heard it, expressed no response to Richard's comment. She closed the heavily embossed Bible, laying one hand reverently upon it as she snapped shut the metal clasps. She arose from the chair, lifted the Bible slowly in both hands, placed it with utmost care next to the defunct radio then returned to her seat. 'I doubt you two will want to join me in prayer,' she remarked, 'but today is the Lord's day and prayer there shall be.'

Closing her eyes, Mrs. Baxendale placed her hands together in devout supplication and in monotone mumbling, offered her thanks to heaven for her life, for the farm and for the food set out before them. Richard glanced at the knife resting next to his plate and wondered if he could inflict a fatal blow on Grimshaw because at present the man had his head bowed, seemingly in deference to Mrs. Baxendale's Sunday ritual. A glimmer of hope might have arisen the previous evening but now was now. Richard's right hand lay flat on the table next to the knife. His fingers splayed and flexing hard against the wooden surface. It should only take a moment. Only a moment and he could seize the knife, lunge forward, thrust the blade deep into Grimshaw's neck then heave the table over against the woman before she was able to take up the shotgun.

Grimshaw raised his head slowly to confirm his eyes were no longer closed but were focused upon the table and therefore on the cutlery. Then they were fixed upon Richard. Richard had observed more than once how agile Grimshaw could be. The table also was solid and heavy and the woman's shotgun, propped up close to her chair, would doubtless be loaded. Karen, her thoughts in limbo, became aware of Grimshaw raising his head further to stare now at her so she kept her own attention firmly upon her plate. Richard noted what was happening as the oblivious Mrs. Baxendale continued her verbal devotions. Lightly tapping outspread fingers on the table, he again glanced at the knife. The knife, so very close. Richard stopped

212

tapping, pulled back his hand and peered about the room.

When Mrs. Baxendale's prayers were done, they were informed it was now time to eat. There followed a charged silence punctuated by what to Karen soon became an irritating clash and screech of knife and fork against plate, an unbearably discordant sound seemingly amplified minute-by-minute, its only counterpoint an occasional spit or crack as logs settled to gasp a renewed flaring in the fireplace. Grimshaw, with half-eaten food dropping now and then from his disfigured mouth as he attempted to chew, continued much of the time to glance bright-eyed at Karen who wished only for time itself to accelerate and bring the ordeal to a merciful conclusion.

With the meal almost ended, Richard asked Mrs. Baxendale, 'How long d'you think you can keep all this going – I mean whether we're forced to help you with jobs around the place or not?' He thought it better not to raise the subject of her age but considered she must be in her early to mid-seventies.

'I'll know when my time comes,' she replied bluntly, clattering down her knife and fork. 'I'll know when the Lord above calls me, but it will not be for some time yet.'

'Just thought I'd ask,' he muttered as in his thoughts hovered the words, 'Presumably when the candles, soap and your other stuff runs out. Or maybe God'll reward you with a coronary.'

The meal was finished. Karen arose to clear the table, reaching across first to where Mrs. Baxendale

213

sat but keeping her eyes fixed resolutely upon the dishes. Richard, aware she would not dare to place her hands near the ever staring, ever menacing Grimshaw, collected up the other plates and cutlery then followed her into the kitchen. The food dropped by Grimshaw onto the table would have to wait although Mrs. Baxendale appeared not to have noticed it. In the kitchen Richard whispered to Karen, 'The key – any chance I could grab it now?'

'Not now,' hissed Karen, glancing aside at the cupboard where the tin containing what they hoped would be the means of their salvation lay. 'It's too risky. I'll wait until later or until she takes him with you to the stable or back to his own place, then I'll - .'

'I'll not 'ave you two in there conspirin'!' rasped the voice from beyond the kitchen then Mrs. Baxendale's face, spectacles glinting, appeared around the door. 'There's no need for two of you in there.' On his return to the main room Mrs. Baxendale said to Richard, 'Now we've eaten I shall read passages to Grimshaw from the Good Book as I do each and every Sunday afternoon. I some'ow doubt your girl will want to 'ear the Lord's truth but when she's finished washin' up int' kitchen you may both sit with us. Otherwise, as there's nowt else to be done on the Sabbath, we'll 'ave to see you back int' stable first.'

Richard looked from one to the other, forced a smile and replied, 'well I'm truly grateful for your offer but I think I'll opt for the stable as long as Karen is soon to join me.'

214

'Very well then - you send 'er back to wait in 'ere with me while you do your necessaries int' utility and I'll 'ave Grimshaw conduct you over there as and when you're done. The girl must remain to finish 'er jobs int' kitchen an' see to takin' out ash an' puttin' more wood ont' fire. She'll do what she 'as to do then join you around sunset with the evenin' meal.'

Richard glanced at the spider-fingered clock on her mantlepiece. There was still much of the afternoon ahead. He looked at the woman, then pointedly at the silently muttering, head-swaying Grimshaw. Mrs. Baxendale appeared to guess his concern over Karen and added, 'Until then I'll keep an eye on things.'

**

The iron bar grated. The door shuddered open and three figures stood against the muted light of a cloud scattered evening. Richard had risen from his bed of straw to approach Karen as she, a tray gripped in both hands, entered the stable. As the door closed and the bar rumbled back, Richard stood before her and said, 'Ah, room service – whatever next.' But there was no humour in his words as he took the tray from her. He peered through the slit between the doors and both stood listening until they were satisfied Mrs Baxendale and Grimshaw no longer loitered outside. They stepped across to the straw beds where Richard placed the tray down onto the floor and in a lowered voice he asked, 'Are you all right? Did you get the keys?'

215

'I took one of the keys,' Karen answered in a half whisper. 'God, Richard, I almost didn't manage it, I almost didn't, and she – she very nearly caught me because of him. I'd no chance of getting my things from the upstairs room either, not with her hanging around the house and the ogre not far away. You were right – it makes more sense to forget about my other stuff.'

'So what happened in there?' he asked, much aware of the anxiety in her voice and seeing in semi-darkness how her hands trembled. 'Was it Grimshaw – did he try to -?'

'Get on with your food and I'll tell you about that in a minute,' she replied, dipping a hand into her coat pocket to produce in deepening gloom the object of their desires. 'I took the key with the remote controller but I left the spare one in there in case she looks inside the tin. If she does and if she sees that she may think both keys are still there among all her other bits and pieces. Trouble is that the remote controller is pretty obvious and she must have used it when she brought the car over here because I already tried the doors and they were locked.'

'Okay but hopefully she won't look,' said Richard, lowering himself onto his makeshift bed where he leaned against the wall and began to eat, adding, 'You hang onto that key until we're ready. At least I managed to get a couple of hours sleep stuck in here on my own.'

Karen sat close by him and said, 'To save you asking, my locket's now in my shoulder bag and I'm hoping it will bring us luck because I tell you,

Richard, something has to. A while after you left with Grimshaw she followed me to the greenhouse when I took out the bucket of ashes. She had to in case he was hanging around out there but it was as if she suspected something else as well because when we got back to the kitchen she stood there all the time watching me until he was back inside the house.'

'I'd hoped the poor bugger would have forgotten all about me going down into the quarry,' breathed Richard, 'but no. On the way over here he grinned at me two or three times and said, "Secret," so what happened over there is still rattling around in his skull. If he repeated it to her then maybe that's got her wondering and that's why she was keeping her eye on you.'

'Well I didn't actually hear him say anything like that to her,' assured Karen. 'After I'd put wood on the fire and gone back to finish in the kitchen, I could hear her getting him to repeat lines from her Bible. When she'd finished, I heard her tell him to wait while she went upstairs for something or other. I thought that would be a good time to reach up for that tin and get the key as she wouldn't hear the cupboard door open or the tin rattle. That tin rattling is what I'd been afraid of, Richard – I mean, *really* afraid. I got the thing down and I took the key out. I was about to put it back inside the cupboard when the door flew open and that foul brute of a man came in mouthing the same words he usually does when he stares at me. I knew what he wanted but I had to get the tin back in there and have the door shut before she came down. I just but only just managed it. I was trying to get the key into my pocket when he grabbed my right arm so hard, I thought he was going to break it. I screamed – I screamed as loud as I could but he wouldn't let go of me. He was holding me, hurting me a lot and trying to rip my clothes and I was struggling so hard I dropped the key. It was then I heard her thumping down the stairs. He had me pressed against the cupboard door and was slavering like a damned great dog when she dashed in and ordered him off. At first, he ignored her and I really thought he was going to push her away or – or knock her down. She kept tugging and tugging at him, shouting and telling him how he'd be punished by God if he didn't do as she said. Once she'd persuaded him to let go of me, I managed to stick my foot over the key but she glared at me as if what had happened was all my fault.'

'One occasion when the Lord came in handy,' remarked Richard. 'Pity the Almighty wasn't around here when the car got stuck.'

'Yes, well, I managed to pick up the key and shove it into my pocket while she was trying to get him out of the kitchen and through to the back door. After she'd locked up there she walked past me without another word and left me alone for a while. I managed to clean up in the kitchen, do the food then get myself sorted out in the back before she poked her nose in again. Before we left the house she started on at me and made out we weren't doing all we were supposed to be doing, especially you – and she mentioned that bloody generator again. When they brought me here he followed really close

218

behind, muttering to himself and I could feel him staring at me all the time. Richard, if we don't get away from this dreadful place soon that brute will go for me and she won't be able to stop him – I know it and I'd rather die than -!'

'Well neither of us is going to die just yet; not if I can help it,' he asserted, picking up the last piece of cheese. He gulped the remaining water from his glass, placed the tray back onto the floor and reached to feel about beneath the straw mattress, saying, 'Ah, got it.' He arose and stood close by her. 'I have the hacksaw blade. Did you get me something to wrap around it?'

'Yes, here in my pocket but it's just an old washing up cloth. I hope that will do.'

'It'll do fine,' Richard assured her, discarding his heavy coat, pushing the saw blade and cloth into his back pocket then kissing her. 'How's your arm now?' he asked.

'Bruised and hurting quite a lot,' she replied. 'I'll have a go but I don't think I'll be too much use helping with that saw.'

'Never you mind. Hang on a minute while I grab my jacket.' He made his way across the stable, now in almost total darkness, laid hands upon the jacket, pulled it on and called across to her, 'Right, let's get busy on those doors. Hang onto your shoulder bag and bring my case over as well.' Richard crossed the stable to where Karen now waited by doors that rattled intermittently in the breeze. He wound the cloth around the intact end of the hacksaw blade and Karen stood by, her a hand on his shoulder as he inserted the blade between the doors.

'D'you think the saw will reach out far enough?' she asked, anxiously.

'Yes,' he breathed. 'Trouble is the doors are so thick I can't get more than three or four inches of blade through to the outside. I'm going to try sawing from the bottom up, I think that'll make it easier because I can get more leverage. During the day, I could see the bar through the gap. I used the blade to make a small notch in the wood, one corresponding with the top of the bar and another for the bottom. I can feel them both with my finger. It should tell us how we're getting on.'

'Careful with your hands,' she said. 'Don't cut yourself.'

'No, it's okay, I think I've wrapped enough cloth around the thing to avoid that. It's going to take quite a while though; that bar looked pretty solid.'

'Will the light from my mobile phone help?' she asked.

'I don't think so, not really - and it's best not to use that until we're away from here in case it gets low on charge.'

Richard, one foot against the left-hand door to prevent it moving, began to saw, slowly at first, back and forth, back and forth, testing the feel of the blade then speeding up. The sound of metal working against metal seemed worryingly amplified through the near empty space of the stable.

Little time had gone by before Karen asked, 'What if the saw breaks? What if he's out there and hears us?'

'What if - what if – what if,' he responded to the rhythm of his hands working the blade. 'If I'm careful, it won't break but if I'm too careful I'll never get through the bar before morning. Tell you what, though; if this works I'm going to take up D.I.Y.'

Richard continued his task with his and Karen's heart beating to the rasp of the saw blade.

'Watch you don't cut yourself,' she repeated.

Richard worked on, pausing occasionally to rest his aching hands.

'How well is it going?' she asked after a long silence. 'Are we going to get out of here?'

'We bloody well have to,' he breathed, pausing momentarily. 'If we don't get out tonight I've a definite feeling we never will.'

As he worked away at the bar Karen recalled once again the sunlit hills and vineyards of Languedoc, the house and gardens and the secluded seat by the pine trees where she would sometimes sit alone to read within sight of the blue Mediterranean. The vision faded when he stopped for another break and she asked, 'Richard, what's the time? I can't see my watch in the dark.'

'What the bloody hell does it matter *what* the time is,' he responded angrily, 'as long as I cut through this damned thing well before daylight!'

'I'm sorry, Richard,' she breathed, 'I just wish I could do something to help - anything.'

'No, love,' he sighed, 'I'm sorry for being a bit short with you. There's nothing you can do to help other than being here and talking to me and that's what I really do appreciate. Let me check the time. Blast - this watch isn't as luminous as it was earlier but it looks to be getting on for nine-thirty. Hm, we've a rough idea what time it starts to get light around here so if the sky's clear I reckon we've less than eight hours to finish the job. If only this blade was longer.' He continued sawing relentlessly, quicker now. The metallic rasping of the blade was their music of hope but at the same time they feared it might serve only as an alarm call should anyone be close outside. That anyone being Grimshaw.

Later on he stopped and said, 'Karen, I have to lay off for a few more minutes. Cloth or no, this damn saw blade is chewing into my fingers. From the feel of it I have to be at least a quarter of the way through.' Scrutinising his watch he added, 'I can hardly tell but I think it's getting on for eleven o'clock. Let's sit down for a while. Better still, why don't you try and get a bit of sleep? I had mine earlier, didn't I.'

'No way, Richard, I couldn't possibly do that while you're working to get us out of here.' They relocated the mattresses and there they sat and talked, but when Richard looked again at his watch the luminosity had declined to a point where the time was no longer readable. 'I must have wasted at least quarter of an hour,' he said at last. 'Let's get busy. There's no going back now, whatever happens. If we don't get through by the time they show up she's bound to see where I've cut through that bar even if he doesn't. And that wailing noise has started outside again – can you hear it?'

'Yes I can hear it but I don't suppose it matters right now.'

Richard renewed his efforts, his breath now and again matching each stroke of the blade. Karen offered occasional encouragement but she knew how much discomfort the work was causing him and suggested again later that he should stop for another rest. Once more they sat but conversed sparingly, almost in whispers. He resumed with the blade after what seemed too long an interval and Karen asked, 'How is it doing, Richard? Can you tell how far you still have to go?'

'God, if you'd asked me that an hour or more back, I'd have said I'd be almost there by now. I can't be too far off, I really can't. I'm running the blade up and down the cut again now and – and yes, it feels like I'm at least three quarters of the way through. Dammit, I have to be, don't I!' He resumed his task and Karen listened to the tireless rasping of the saw, punctuated every so often by a few seconds of tense silence until Richard said, 'I'll take another rest before my hand packs up completely but this will have to be the last.'

They sat a while but said little until Richard, flexing his fingers, arose and, followed by Karen, felt his way back to the doors. He worked on but by then they could no more than guess how much time had passed. Karen stepped aside to look up at the window, hoping there would be no sign yet of impending dawn. That small part of the sky open to her had cleared and stars were visible so she returned to Richard's side and assured him, 'It's definitely still night-time – it's pitch dark out there and the sky's clear.'

He paused a few seconds to take a deep breath, saying, 'But not for very much longer I suspect; I have to get through this thing soon, don't I.' He continued with renewed vigour, adding, 'It just cannot-cannot-cannot take much longer,' But it seemed only minutes had passed when he stopped again to mutter impatiently, 'Oh, the damned blade's stuck.' He hesitated, tugged, tugged again, this time harder, but the blade still would not move. He cursed under his breath then wrenched hard to free it. A sharp crack and Richard gasped, 'Oh, Christ - the bloody thing's snapped!' He pulled back and they heard a ping as the broken section of the blade landed outside the doors.

Silence, then Karen asked dryly, 'Is - is that it?'

Richard stared at the narrow gap between the doors for some moments then placed his hand on her shoulder, saying, 'I was almost through so what's left of the bar might give. Get against the doors. When I say - heave as hard as you can. We have to try.'

Both pushed hard with Karen avoiding pressure on her painful right arm. The doors creaked, flexed and rattled but the bar would not give. Karen breathed, 'Richard, what else can we do?'

Richard stepped back, called aloud in angered frustration, 'I'll not give up - not now I won't!' and kicked with an echoing thud of his boot against the timbers.

'Richard, don't!' she pleaded, 'they'll hear us. It'll make things worse.'

'They can't get any worse!' he exclaimed, laying a hand against one of the doors then, 'Hey - wait! Karen that did it - the bar's broken!' He pushed the left-hand door and it moved slightly open. From the gap, Richard peered across to the main house then turned to Karen. 'There's no sign of life out there and the place is in darkness.'

'We're lucky her geese didn't start up,' whispered Karen.

Richard pushed harder, the door swung lazily out and they were bathed by chill night air. Beneath the lowering three-quarter moon a damp, dense mist drifted close above the ground. Richard picked up his case. Karen gripped tightly on her shoulder bag.

'Give me that key,' he hissed. 'Let's get moving.'

'Richard,' she responded, fumbling in her pocket then handing him the key, 'what if they've done something to the car and it won't start?'

'I can't see why either of 'em would or even could - and like I said, we have no choice.'

They stepped warily out. The mist for a time intensified, obscuring then revealing already to the east a horizon that bore, between the visible peaks, a faintest blush of morning. They hesitated until the vapour passed as a shroud between themselves and the house. The air still carried that mournful dirge they knew well; it seemed to mock them as they moved at first cautiously, then with quicker steps away from the stable and toward the rear of the house. Karen peered at the main house as the mist thinned once more. 'Richard, there's a lamp on in there,' she whispered, grasping his arm. 'There's someone moving about. It must be her. Let's hope she didn't hear you kick the doors.'

'Forget it,' he hissed, 'just keep going and watch you don't trip on anything.'

They continued on, stooping low, their steps unsure as they splashed through black pools of water, hearts pounding, breath fogging before their faces in the cold air. They were over halfway across open ground when the noises began; a raucous honking, a tocsin fit to awaken the spirits of the surrounding hills. 'It's those bloody geese!' he exclaimed, 'faster - we can't stop now!'

On they stumbled as, passing the side of the house, they saw the lamp move aside. At the window a face appeared.

'She's seen us!' Karen gasped. 'Richard, she's seen us!'

'Just keep going,' he urged, 'we're almost there.'

Within pounding heartbeats of the car, Richard pressed the remote-control button on the key. They knew the external lights of the car would flash on and off but that did nothing to diminish the shock of seeing their own presence so blatantly advertised. They reached the car, wrenched open the doors, frantically tossed shoulder bag and case over the front seat headrests and into the back. The car's interior lights had sprung on to create an all-betraying floodlit stage as Richard and Karen fell into their seats. The rear door of the main house swung open and Karen glimpsed Mrs Baxendale illuminated by the light of an oil lamp she held high as the car doors slammed shut. As the figure vanished, Richard, in fumbling desperation, fitted and turned the key.

'Richard,' Karen gasped, 'she's gone back in there. She's gone for the gun!'

The headlights glared to illuminate the mist, the engine burst into life as he thrust the gear lever into position. The engine howled and with tyres spitting grit, the car lurched forward bouncing, careering in the direction of the vaguely visible dirt track with the seat belt warning signal letting out an insistent warble. Crossing wet grass, the wheels lost, gained then once more lost traction to Richard's muttered curses. The tyres regained their grip. Richard swerved onto the dirt track, turning left along the side of the house then slewing left once more to gain speed and pass across the front. Mrs Baxendale appeared, illuminated by their headlights as she stepped from the main door and darted into their path with her shotgun raised.

'Get your head down!' shouted Richard as he careered on causing Mrs Baxendale to lurch out of the way before she could fire directly at them. Karen squeezed low then moments later cried out as the rear window disintegrated explosively with lead-shot and glass fragments spattering throughout the car. His head also lowered to avoid the blast, Richard had braked instinctively but the car stalled. Murmuring further curses he restarted and had the engine revving hard. They were surging forward again when from the mist before them a spade-wielding figure sprang out from the darkness into the glare of their headlights. Karen clasped hands to her face as Grimshaw loomed large, his eyes gleaming, his spade raised high to smash through the windscreen. Richard accelerated hard. The engine roared. A violent thud shook the car but still they drove on. 'Ohhhh!' cried Karen, bracing her hands against the dashboard as the spade clang-clattered over the car roof and Grimshaw's bloodied, twisted face, mouth agape, adhered itself to the windscreen with his eyes staring into hers. Richard braked hard, the car skidded to a halt and Grimshaw's sprawling bulk, arms akimbo, slid quivering from the bonnet. Richard gritted his teeth and accelerated forward once more, the car pitching violently as it impacted and jolted over their fallen assailant. But now they were ascending the curved track away from the house.

Numbed with shock, fingers spread about her face, Karen stared ahead as they approached the clearing, already having passed the grass embankment where on that fateful night she had waited alone for Richard's return. 'Oh, god at last we're out of there,' she moaned. 'At long, long last we're free.'

'Yes,' muttered Richard, 'and it looks like that nasty old bitch lost her handyman today as well as her two slaves.'

At the clearing he took great care to avoid the spot where they had earlier become mired, negotiating the firmer, drier ground at the periphery at as higher speed as he dared, passing the lane that once accessed the quarry before reaching the inconspicuous but welcoming exit. They continued along the rough, partly obstructed track to the pot-holed side road then, in the half-light of dawn, they emerged onto the main road where people were headed for work at the start of the Monday rush hour. Here was a scene so familiar, a scene so very ordinary, often stressful for some, yet the busy highway was to Richard and Karen at that moment a vision of golden paradise. They continued slowly along the inside lane with headlights flashing and horns blaring aloud from passing vehicles. Richard eased onto the roadside grass verge, slowed to a standstill, pulled on the brake and stabbed at a button below the dashboard. 'We've no hazard lights and I guess we don't have rear lights either.' He pulled open the glove compartment, saying, 'Let's try my phone – it's still here. Let's see if we can get anything.' He withdrew the phone, switched on and stabbed at the keys. 'The damned signal is still too weak,' he informed her.

Unencumbered by her seat belt, Karen reached behind for her bag, withdrew her phone and tried likewise. 'No,' she said, 'I get nothing either.'

'Okay,' he declared, putting the car back into gear, 'then I'll carry on until we find an emergency phone, a house, anything. There has to be something along here sooner or later.'

Karen dropped her phone into her bag, lay back in her seat, pressed hands against her cheeks, closed her eyes and was now aware of cold air entering from the shattered rear window. More blaring horns, more flashing lights from passing motorists meant very little to her. 'I can't believe it,' she sighed. 'I can't believe who or where I am any more. No, Richard, I can't.'

'We're well away from that madhouse and safe now,' he responded, 'and that's all that matters. Look, here's a lay-by; I'm pulling over and we'll see if my phone works when I plug into the USB. If not then we'll just have to go on further.'

A yellow and blue police vehicle passed slowly by as they drew to a halt. It slowed further, pulled in ahead of them, reversed and stopped close in front of their car. A uniformed figure emerged. With the engine still running, Richard lowered the window. The officer approached while his colleague could be heard on their radio, calling up, Richard assumed, to check on their car.

The first officer paused to assess a broken headlight and impact damage at the front then moved to the side of the car, his face large at the window to ask, 'Is anyone hurt, sir? Your car appears to have suffered considerable damage.'

'No, we're not hurt,' Richard replied, 'and no, we've not been in any kind of accident.'

'And is this your vehicle, sir?' he asked as the second officer appeared at his side.

'It's a hire car, or what's left of it,' replied Richard, switching off the engine. The officer moved back as Richard opened the door to clamber out. 'Christ,' he breathed, 'I never thought I'd be so glad to see the police.'

Karen, too, eased herself from the car and stepped around to stand by Richard.

The second officer exchanged a few words with the first, looked briefly at the front of the car, moved around to inspect the rear then returned to his colleague. Both regarded with undisguised curiosity the two disarrayed and oddly attired figures as the second officer declared in the mandatory tone of officialdom, 'We will need to take a few details from you. Meanwhile, sir, this vehicle would appear to be in an unroadworthy condition *and* without working rear lights?'

'You're quite right, officer,' smiled Richard, 'no rear lights at all and that is quite inexcusable. We do have an explanation though, if you have time to spare before giving us a lift to the police station. After that we look forward to giving you a full and detailed statement. Oh, and I may have run over someone a short time ago – quite unintentionally, I assure you.'

Karen clasped hands once more to her face and leaned against the car saying, 'Yes, I assure you the car was perfectly all right until a few minutes ago - really it was.' Then as the threads of tension and fear unravelled, she began to laugh.

***

Little time passed before the local press and radio had a lurid tale to tell. Outside the once thought abandoned Lower Moss Farm, police had come upon the part crushed body of a badly disfigured but unidentified male. Inside the main house they had discovered the gruesome remains of an elderly woman, killed by the blast of a shotgun placed inside her mouth. Beside her had lain a large, blood-soaked, family bible and on the mantelpiece above a blood and brain-spattered antique clock ticked away the minutes and hours in blind indifference. On entering an outbuilding by the ash trees they had been confronted by a decayed male corpse, fully dressed and seated next to a vase of slightly wilted flowers. Within a shattered car at the bottom of the nearby quarry they came upon two broken bodies; the remains of a middle-aged couple reported as missing almost two years earlier.

***

In the wide loneliness of night, when land and sky breathed elemental voices, the singing stones gave mournful elegy to the valley below. Within the deserted farm, within its chill, empty rooms were sighs and clicks as breeze and rain touched about the windows. And when shrouding mists possessed the valley, when the winds had calmed, there reigned profound silence. Within darkened corners of the house were unseen realms of small restless creatures that meandered from nowhere to nowhere, predator and scavenging prey in silent, deadly contest. And in the darkest corner of the kitchen, close to the cold iron stove, the voracious black spider, patient but ever alert, awaited whichever of these unsuspecting creatures might fall within her reach.

THE END

My many thanks to Lynda Buxton for spotting and correcting my text errors.

Other novels by this author

The Devil in Eden
The Man Who Sought Eternity
Return of The Hero
Shadow of The Beast

Further works by Jeff Clarke may be found on

www.jeffreypeterclarke.co.uk

And on his author page at:
https://fiction4all.com/ebooks/a1549.htm

www.ingramcontent.com/pod-product-compliance
Lightning Source LLC
Chambersburg PA
CBHW070926180626
46817CB00003B/1209